D1392611

ZADE

Heather Reyes

ZADE

SAQI

British Library Cataloguing-in-Publication Data
A catalogue for this book is available from the
British Library

ISBN 0 86356 534 4

copyright © 2004 Heather Reyes

This edition first published 2004

*The right of Heather Reyes to be identified as the author of this work has been asserted
by her in accordance with the Copyright, Designs and Patents Act of 1988*

Page 120: illustration from: Apollinaire, *Calligrammes*,
© NRF, Gallimard, Paris: 2001, p. 102

Page 147: excerpts from: *Break on Through* and *The End*,
© The Doors, 1967

Saqi Books
26 Westbourne Grove
London W2 5RH

www.saqibooks.com

> *For some people dead is dead*
> *and for some people dead is not dead.*
> After Gertrude Stein

In films it's usually through the temple. Or the mouth.

Transfer the gun to the right hand. Release the safety catch.

… Come on … just do it …

Unfamiliar smell of metal and grease. The taste …

No – not the mouth. Pink and ivory cave of words and breathing.

Straight through the brain – through the grey mess.

Arm trembling. Raising it. So heavy. Left hand pulls back the hood. Sudden chill air around the ears and the back of the neck. Shiver. Trying to hold steady. The circle of metal against the skin of the temple where that little blue vein trembles just below the surface – level with the right eye.

Curve of the trigger against the finger. Shaking …

Sense of unreality about it all. Life – death –

Oh, this living business … this dying business … Just get it *over* with. *Now* –

Blast of blinding light …

White light blown apart into its seven colours – now merging to white again. Stare of a blank white page wanting words. Then the brightness fading, shrinking to a pinpoint. Darkness. Inky black fills the page. A page written over so many times with so many words, layer on layer of other people's words until, no word or letter distinct, there's not a wink of white between them. Letters tangled round and through each other: old wool in a tight mess impossible to unravel.

A page of utter black. A place where no light is. Just dark. Dark. Nothing but dark. Suffocation. The oppression of blood with no air so the lungs are bursting with red pain. A shirt of flame. Red … So red …

The shirt of flame no longer hurting now, but flaring up, flickering with the remains of images and words. Watching through the burning redness, watching … An audience to one's own life played out. The central character. Like playing Saint Joan again. ('*These English are impossible: they will thrust her straight into the fire. Look! … The sooner it's over, the better for that poor girl …*')

Seeing it. Contained. Over. A life.

But not the expected whole life replayed, not the whole thing 'flashing before you'. Just the last two hours. Or is chronology scrambled now? Chapter One – 'The End'. The rest later? (Chapters bound in the wrong order.) And this time through a glass, redly. There. Watch. Down there in that red light. Watch …

Edge out of the hiding place, stiff with cold. It's dark. Paris life rumbles by beyond the cemetery walls. Père Lachaise.

So dark. Dark red. Anorak dragging down on both sides. Torch in the right-hand pocket. Take it out. Left-hand side of the coat weighed down with nothing to balance it.

Feel for the torch button. Keep the beam low; don't attract security guards. With snarling Alsatians?

Direct the torchlight straight down. Again that moment of the boot caught in the beam – the boot lit up, so 'there' in the nothingness of the dark. Familiar old boot still with the mud of the Bois de Boulogne on it.

That walk in the Bois when it rained so hard everyone else ran for cover. Hair darkened, flattened with it, rivulets running down the back of the neck. Not caring. Stinging cheeks. Alone. The cold, cold rain.

The last of October. 'Allhallows Eve'. In the torch beam, fallen leaves win back a brief colour from the dark. Narrow path. Ghostly tombs jostling in from either side. Such burdens of stone weigh down the earth. To stop the dead from rising? (Whatever.) Gleams of gold lettering in the dark ...*çois Ducha*... Flickering of names and dates, whole lives of struggle and effort passed over in a flash ... a sparrow flitting through a lighted hall ...

Torch beam low on the path. Cat sliding swiftly through it ... a pair of green sparks flash out of the crimsoned dark.

Sudden noise. Duck down. Turn off the torch. Security guards? Dogs snuffling about?

The slight sound again. Squealing – pitifully small but blood-chilling. A rodent struggling against its death. A cat's hunger met. 'Life'. Appalling.

Sudden urge to 'get it over'. Stumbling back to the path ... and so to Héloïse and Abelard – the 'Romeo and Juliet' tomb (*he* called it that). But not 'star-cross'd lovers' at all – just two clever people who'd had their lives messed up for them by others. Same thing? The perfect place.

Shining the torch across their parallel bodies, the dark stone crevices, expressionless faces. No romantic thoughts. Just an overwhelming need to pee. Keep still and it'll go away.

Sit down, lean against the cold railings round the tomb. The quiet, ten o'clock 'bibbing' muffled under jumper and anorak. Pull back the left sleeve, flash the torch on the watch. Squeal of brakes, screech of tires, horns blaring. City sounds. (Far off. So near.) An ambulance on its way somewhere …

Is it possible to do this thing, after all? … To put a gun to your head not knowing if it's loaded? Not *knowing*?

Insidious whisper of paper taken from the pocket: the letter they would find on her afterwards, if. To be outlasted by a piece of paper, by your written words … Suddenly so sorry for the body. All its marvels. (The biology textbook full of maps – the blood, the nerves, the contours of muscles … That film on human reproduction … And how many million synapses was it in a piece of brain tissue the size of a grain of sand? …)

Cold. Pull up the hood. Clouds clearing from a half-hearted red moon. Unfold the letter. Torchlight on the words. Re-read them, searching for resolve. The neat, close script.

Words, words, words … A final attempt to construct a fragile bridge between them. (Twisted stems knotted into a swaying walkway over a chasm in a far-off, roadless country …)

'*Chers Papa, Madeleine et Pierre …*'

The writing small, more and more unsteady. Hard to read with the torch in such darkness with the wind pulling hair across the face …

And so tired … so very, very tired … Nights and nights with no proper sleep …

Drifting … the irresistible pull of sleep …

… out of which dark well a little bird cheeps – the watch bibbing midnight!

Panic.

The rapid re-run turns to slow motion. Reach slowly … slowly … down – into – the – deep well of the pocket. Slowly … so slowly … drawing out the gun. Loaded? – or not? Death or life. Let the gun do the choosing.

'In films, it's usually through the temple. Or the mouth.'

In slow motion, again transfer the gun – to the right hand and – release the safety catch. (Slow … so slow …) Raise – the – barrel – to – the – open – mouth … rest – it – on – the teeth … smelling, tasting metal and grease. (Then the picture dropping into the mind – mouth as a lovely pink cave … the teeth as sculpted ivory. Precious …) Ugly taste of the gun … Wanting to spit it out …

Not the mouth, then. Slowly, slowly withdraw the dark gun and in a gesture that seems – to – take – all – et-ern-it-y … all – all – et-ern-it-y … – raise it towards the temple while the left hand pulls back the hood. Shivering slowly in the chill red air. Feel again the even colder circle of metal against the skin that seems to only just cover the little blue vein. Curve the finger once more against the trigger … this living business … this dying business … (Whatever.) Just get it over with …

Now –

Staring into the fire. It always seemed to be Christmas at Grandma Robertson's house with the big open fireplace and the neat pyramid of split logs on the left-hand side of the hearth and the rack for the fire-tongs and the poker and the hearth-brush on the right. The fire brought out the resiny smell of the enormous (to me, then) Christmas tree in the corner – the first thing I'd run to see when we'd arrive late in the afternoon of Christmas Eve. A queen tree – with her jewellery of fine glass baubles shining pink and silver and purple and gold in the sprinkled white lights (wires invisible in the darkened room), holding out gifts with the ends of her sweet green fingers and crowned with the same silver star each year – a diadem passed down through the generations of queen trees … Wonderful tree stories in my head. She was Yggdrasil from my *Picture Book of Norse Myths*, her golden baubles were the honey that dropped from those branches that bound together heaven, earth and hell, little white star-lights of the universe scattered among her branches … all muddling itself up in my head with the *Stories from Ovid* and the one I made up where my mother, running from the roaring car-monster, had not really died in the accident: she'd cheated death, fled from the scene, run into a wood and turned into a Christmas tree, her spirit passing from tree to tree down the years to be with me each Christmas … which was fine until the year I was ill and we had to stay on until Twelfth Night and from my pillowy bed on the sofa I watched Grandma strip the queen of her jewels, pack them away into old biscuit boxes and then (the horror of it!) chop the naked tree into little pieces with red secateurs and feed her, piece by piece, into the fire … Wanting to cry out … My voice strangled in my swollen throat …

Just the day before, Uncle Edward had seen me squatting close to the fire and gazing into it (there were palaces lit by incredible orange sunsets … magical grottoes with luminous gold walls …) and he'd said, 'See the fiery caves between the coals? They're full of little devils waiting to hurt you – so never go too near the fire. See those sparks when I poke the fire even a little bit? – like that? They're tiny devils jumping out of the caves, furious I've disturbed their home. They're trying to get at my hand and burn it …'

Burning … Burning ….

Devils. Hellfire. The preacher in the strange church visited once – only once – with Aunt Berthe, to please her. The preacher so vivid on what would happen to sinners if … The pain of skin blistering and peeling away from raw flesh, of inner organs sizzling, exploding, eyes melting … Nightmares. Red nightmares …

But useful later for playing Saint Joan. 'Unnervingly convincing', my English teacher said to me afterwards. 'You really made the audience share Joan's agonies – the spiritual and the physical. I didn't think you had it in you … I had no idea you …'

I'd simply thought of what the preacher said ... and my mother trapped in a burning car...

But the pictures fade and all that's left is ...

The gun at the head and burning ... burning ...

A head full of burning. An empty scream.

Listen.

Look.

Great orange tongues leap and flicker – stifled cries fill the burning air ... Straight to hell, then?

Looking into fiery light, the sensation of being sucked forward in time – *part* of me sucked forward, while the root of me remains anchored there, heavy on the ground. Stretched and stretched (that scene from the film with the man on the rack ...) – till the pull is too much and there's a split into the me cold and small and young on the ground, and the me that has hurtled forward into a time, an age, a state of mind not yet inhabited. How else to describe it? Both in myself and watching myself – this broken-off part of myself seeming older. Wiser? – not necessarily, but seeing things from a different angle.

The part of myself that has broken away from that girl on the ground is waiting, curious to see what will happen. My whole brain curves itself into a question mark.

But something is beginning. The cries and hissing whispers turn to voices that jabber out of the flames, gabbling, muttering, tongues confused (half-remembered story of Babel). Voices scolding, mocking, accusing ... What do they want with me? What can I say?

As from a prompt box I hear the word 'sorry'. So that's it.

The required words come into my mouth.

'I'm sorry, Papa – I didn't mean it …'

'I'm sorry, Grandma – I didn't know it would …'

'I'm sorry, Lucien …'

'Driss, I'm so sorry …'

'Please, everyone, forgive me.'

Almost at once the orange flames brighten and lighten to blinding gold. (The early sun on the sea that morning in Nice. The word 'glory'.) Figures begin to form in the floodlight of yellowness, yellow themselves. Who are these people?

They draw nearer, grow more distinct, more solid. Imagined? – or seen? Outside the head? – or inside?

But I'm simply dazzled, amazed to see golden flames turn to quivering sunflower petals, collect themselves into great round blooms, arrange themselves in a Van Gogh vase – then lose their definition as they melt to a sun-flood of gold.

Gold. Such gold!

In the dazzle of it (early sun on the bay that morning, great dish of trembling, liquid light), the schizophrenic vision deepens. Both in myself and watching myself. Yes, I am – or seem to be – some aspect of myself, yet quite separate from that slumped little creature down there. I feel so sorry for her. I want to touch that pale inside of her thin wrist with its delta of veins. They look so strange, as if I've never seen them before. Is there a pulse? I listen for the slow drumbeat of my heart. But all I hear is the shuffle of feet.

Figures edging forward out of the golden light. I see the worried looks on their faces as they first catch sight of the girl propped against the railings – a small thing in big boots and over-large anorak.

They see the gun in her right hand, resting on the ground beside her. No one moves forward to touch her.

After a few moments, a voice – somehow surprising in its soft clarity – comes out of the buttery brightness. 'Are you all right, Mam'selle?'

No answer.

The voice tries again, more insistently. 'Mam'selle? Are you all right?'

Her bowed head is raised, slowly. Faint sighs of satisfaction and relief from the shining figures.

With them I see her pinched, pale face, the eyes confused, but wary and defensive. (The gun not loaded, then? The voice of a gendarme? What will they do to her? To me? Will I have to go on with my life, then? What an effort. What a bore …)

I blink into the brightness.

A small man steps forward: he has a neat moustache, tailored coat, dark, intelligent eyes. Not a gendarme. A familiar face nevertheless … Those lovely eyes. Wasn't there once someone I loved who …? The girl's brow furrows, trying to remember … Is it *him*?

He takes another step towards her, holds out a hand as if to help her to her feet. No – it's not him. She raises the gun, points it at the man's heart.

The little man looks suddenly perplexed at being threatened in this way.

'Mam'selle?'

'Leave her, leave her.' (A woman's voice. American?) The man retreats into the golden, ghostly crowd.

Still training the gun on them, she struggles shakily to her feet. 'Who are you?' She narrows her eyes, trying to see them.

'And why's the sun so bright? It can't be morning already. Why's it so bright? I can't see you properly.'

A large figure in a hat and silk cape moves towards her – but she aims the gun at his chest.

'No closer.' (Who *are* they? *What* are they? Phantoms? Real and unreal at the same time. A strange golden carnival. A monochrome crowd shuffling nearer, drenched in blinding light. But whoever they are, I don't want them bothering me now. I don't want anybody. I only want peace. I want to be emptied of everything. Everything.)

'Just go away and leave me alone.'

But they won't go.

She raises her voice and brandishes the gun. 'Did you hear me? I said "go". Anyway, you look silly dressed like that. Are you in a play or something? Well, go back to it!'

The American woman (short, stocky) laughs quietly. (Her laughter, her look … someone I once loved?) 'How strange we must look,' she says. 'How strange. Strange – stranger – strangest …'

'She's not so very *un*strange herself! Those boots! – on a young woman. And her coat's too big. Looks as though it belongs to someone else. It doesn't look quite *right*, somehow…'

Yes, I know. I know that. But it's his. (He lent it to me that day when … I tricked myself into believing the smell of him clung to the seams.)

'… not quite right at all. But what does "strange" matter, anyway?' (The large man in the hat and cape.) 'Strange – stranger – strangest … strange – stranger …'

His voice fades into the twittering of starlings in an afternoon tree, golden afternoon.

The garden of the Normandy house. August. Reading under the tree. A head full of poetry and starlings.

She shakes her head as if to rid it of a buzzing in the ears. (*'The buzzing? ... yes ... all silent but for the buzzing ...'*) Who *is* this happening to? To her, *her*. Not me ... *She* was the one who didn't care if she lived or died. *She* fired the gun, not knowing whether it was loaded ... And now ... it's all so strange and *different*, as if I don't *know* myself. As if I'm dying before I even ... I want to say something, but I don't really know what it is. Will I remember before it's too late? I stare into the light which begins to purify and separate the sounds until I can hear the words distinctly again (*'yes ... the tongue in the mouth ... all those contortions ...'* a mouth wording off in the darkness ...) ... hear the words distinctly, as if from a front-row seat in a theatre. It's the uncomfortable fascination of bad drama – melodrama? comedy? ... or tragicomedy? Whatever it is, I seem to be the leading lady.

The man in the hat and cape is still muttering about strangeness. On and on he goes until the American woman (broadish, kind face – reminding me of someone I once loved ... but not my mother. I never knew her. I wasn't even two years old) ... the American woman says, 'Okay, Oscar. Enough is enough is enough ...'

'Taisez-vous – just shut up, both of you.' (A man with a bandaged head. Again I'm half-way to finding the person I loved. The faces and the voices in my head keep hinting but still I can't quite ... And I want to so much. I want him so much. And the name, the image keeps slipping away, just out of memory. And this bandaged head. It bothers me. I seem to have known so many

injured heads. Damaged bodies. Even my dreams wear bandages. If this *is* a dream. How are we supposed to know whether …?) The mouth of the bandaged head speaks again: 'Just shut up, Oscar. This could be a matter of life and death. Be serious.'

'Oh, come on, Guillaume, life is far too important a thing to ever talk seriously about. And as for death, well …'

But the girl's threatening them with the gun again. (I want to shake her by the shoulders and say, 'Can't you see, silly girl? They're your *friends*.') And she's started shouting at them. And I'm afraid she's going to make an absolute fool of herself. Part of me wants nothing more to do with her.

'Listen, you lot – just PISS OFF. I came here to be alone … probably to die, if you must know. I came here to *die* – possibly.'

I cringe at her cheap melodrama. ('*O Fates, come, come, Cut thread and thrum; Quail, crush, conclude, and … Thus die I, thus, thus, thus …*' But this isn't *A Midsummer Night's Dream*. An 'Allhallows' nightmare, maybe. And if it's only that, only a dream, then … But we don't know. We don't know. Reality, dreams: it's all just electrical charges through the brain, isn't it? Just pictures, sounds. Synapses. Little pricks to the soft grey walnut inside the skull …)

Her melodrama – it's even worse than the others' comedy. And yet I feel for her still: to her it's not cheap, it's not melodrama. She's so young. Twenty. And what else can she say into the glaring yellow? Only 'I came here to die.'

'To die?! Oh, Mam'selle, don't say that!' The little moustachioed man in the big coat again. His chest wheezes as he speaks. 'Don't be anxious for death. Life's so short and death comes of its own accord soon enough.'

'Oh, don't be so banal,' sneers the girl.

The little man looks taken aback. I feel for him. A wave of amusement passes through the others as they stand close together in the cheerful yellow light. The girl is confused, hurt: her violence isn't being taken seriously.

Madeleine – my replacement '*maman*' – insisting on doing my make-up, adjusting my hair, to make me look how she wanted for the party. Me looking in the mirror, seeing a clown. Taking the mirror off the wall and throwing it on the floor. Her laughter. Hating her then more than I'd ever done before. Hating her laughter.

'What are you laughing at? Don't you dare laugh at me.' She brandishes the gun, but her voice and manner are faltering. 'Don't laugh at me … don't laugh …'

'Don't take offence, young lady.' (The one they call Oscar.) 'It's just that, well, one doesn't usually accuse Monsieur Proust of *banality*.'

Their laughter dies as the girl's face registers a succession of contradictory emotions. I, too, struggle to find some kind of 'anchor' for what I've just heard. I stare at the little man with the dark, expressive eyes, reminding me of someone I once …. My mind's working so slowly …

Think.

Think –

Something to do with a book? …

The essay prize. The first time I'd ever won anything. I was thirteen. They presented it to me wrapped in red paper with a gold ribbon around it because it was 'First Prize'. A big book, with pictures. *The History of Literature.* Papa so proud – the special dinner to celebrate ... I read it so often I could quote from it verbatim. And the photographs ... Proust with his head slightly on one side, his finger on his cheek, looking into the camera ... opposite Picasso's portrait of Gertrude Stein.

With a lurch of astonishment I recognise Marcel Proust ... and then the short, stocky American woman: Gertrude Stein. But the two faces seem to merge for a moment (*'The eyes of a familiar compound ghost ...'*) – someone I loved, love. Is it him? (*'The eyes ...'*) But they separate again. (Please don't go! Please don't go!)

I make a huge effort to remember, to bring him back – his face, his name – all I want is to be with him again. Is this hell? – this wanting and wanting and not being able to ... Thinking it's him, then realizing it's someone else? A different kind of loved one. Different kinds of love getting muddled in the head ...

This absence of love, of the loved one, not being able to ...

Come on: try, *try* ... Bring it all back ... Bring it *back* ...

I begin to tremble violently with the effort of it, trying to close my eyes against the glare of the white-gold light which seems to be the reason I can't remember, can't bring back the feeling of him, the reality of him, the reality of my love for him.

The effort's too much. I'm reduced to watching that other part of myself again. That girl there.

She looks on the verge of collapse when figures (conjured by her distress?) appear on either side of her, supporting her into a sitting position once more. Long robes. A man and a woman. The girl puts her head between her knees, as if warding off a faint. She's not moving. Is she dying? Dead?

We're all very quiet, watching.

After a few moments, the woman at her side tries, very gently, to remove the gun from the girl's hand. But she holds on tightly and snaps, 'Don't you dare!', waving the weapon at a rather beautiful nun sculpted from golden light – the embodiment of a spirited intelligence.

'Leave her, Héloïse.' (The authoritative voice of the man.)

Squinting into the brightness, the girl looks from the nun to the man and back to the nun again. I want to laugh, but the girl's face is dissolving into such a mask of incomprehension and fear that it would be a great unkindness even to smile at her distress. She was trying to conjure the man she loved but …

It's old Peter Abelard beside her.

'I can't tell what's happening … I think I'm going to be sick … Help me! …'

Héloïse bends over her and places a cool golden hand on her forehead. Gertrude Stein comes slowly to her, kneels, with difficulty, beside the girl and puts a plump, warm-gold arm around her shoulders: comfort. At this moment it's her deepest wish. *My* deepest wish. To be comforted. Not self-pity, exactly. Just a need to be – comforted.

With this comfort, the loved one begins to come back to me – though not happily, because the last time comfort was offered to me – was …

Comfort from the arms of strangers: the arms around me were mostly those I'd never touched before. Everyone trying – though, really, there was no comfort at all.

I close my eyes again, though the brightness still shines through my eyelids. Then the words, when they come, are squeezed from the deepest, most terrified part of myself.

'Am – I – dead … or – not?'

A long pause.

No reply.

I close my eyes.

'I'm frightened. Help me – *please* …'

The yellow glare gentles to a lucid green that has in it the lovely juice of all the springs I've ever known. Apple-green, pea-green, grass-green – after the spring rain a glimmering emerald light … Everything alive with it. Green. Colour of life.

It's as the light turns to green that the effort to remember – to re-create us together – is repaid. Sharp return of memories. Though it's bitter-sweet. Having him and not having him. Half-light of a remembered life. A kind of hell. Purgatory, at least.

I'd turned seventeen in February. I met Driss in March. In May we became lovers. The air was warm, but not that summer-hot that makes the city stink and the air unbreathable with car-fumes. And there were flowers. I'd never noticed so many flowers before. He laughed at me – said they'd always been there. But then I'm used to being laughed at – me with my long, serious face and my glasses and my legs like twigs. When he made fun of me, though, it was just a kind of playful tenderness. He never laughed at me for being quiet, for my books, for liking to do things other people my age didn't often bother with. Pierre always sneered at me for going to galleries, theatres, museums. He'd turn up his rock music whenever I tried to practise the flute. And Madeleine never said a word. And my father had to be careful, of course. Pierre wasn't so thick that he couldn't detect the closeness between us – Papa and me – the way we could just be quiet together.

But I could talk all right when there was something worth saying. I was in the drama group at school. It was easier to be confident when you weren't playing yourself. I even played Saint Joan when they put on Shaw's version – though in French, of course. I think they chose me because I looked a bit plain and boyish. I remember my father telling me the English call the *foyer d'artistes* the Green Room – I remember it because for that play the entire cast was made to wear blood-red costumes by our eccentric Mademoiselle Dubois from the art department. So the Green Room was full of blood and fire. Red and green: colours in opposition.

I'd always been very aware of colour – even when I was very small, my father said. I hated mustard yellow and used to cry if he tried to cuddle me while wearing his mustard-coloured pullover. My favourite colour was blue. Pale blue. 'The colour of idealism,' my father used to say. 'You'll be condemned to disappointment, I'm afraid, my lamb …'

I used to think I'd like to be an artist. I was good – but not good enough. The pictures I'd been brought up with were reproductions of rather tedious eighteenth- and early nineteenth-century stuff hung in curly gilt frames in our hall and dining-room. And at school they used to put up abstract things – geometric shapes in primary colours or black and white or scribbly Jackson Pollocks. They were supposed to appeal to us. But they didn't really do anything for me. Matisse, Picasso, Cézanne, Braque, Kandinsky … they were the ones I loved – their ways of seeing things, their enthusiasm for life, their appreciation of the ordinary and their courage. When I looked at a plate of apples painted by Cézanne, I felt the preciousness of a passing moment of life and saw real apples more intensely, more completely. The curves and planes of a Braque helped me grasp the geometry behind the fluid surfaces of things, made me feel calm, reassured; and Picasso – all that energy and diversity and strangeness, yet familiar emotions … and Kandinsky with his arrangements of our 'iridescent chaos' – which is what Cézanne said we were – and …

Mademoiselle Dubois teased me for being old-fashioned – 'all that old Modernist stuff'. I tried to explain I liked the way they didn't ignore the ordinary things of human life – the way it wasn't all geometry or satirical statements or whatever her preferred kind of art was. It was people in geometry, if you like, and geometry in people and their things. It was a coming together of so many ideas, visions. But I gave up trying to put it into words for her. I wasn't even sure I understood it myself. Anyway, she would have laughed at me no matter what I said. It was what everyone did.

I didn't just look at the pictures. I read about the artists and their lives, lived them in my head. They were more interesting than my own. I filled whole notebooks with my own shape poems – 'Calligrammes' (Apollinaire was my hero for a while) – and pieces of writing that were spread out in huge letters at one point and bunched into tiny, close lines elsewhere. Art and writing coming together. (Perhaps I'd be a writer …) And then, of course, Proust. That time I buried myself in the first volume they nicknamed me '*la fille perdue*', and Pierre kept making feeble jokes about me 'losing my time'. Whatever I did was a waste of time to him. He was poisoned by jealousy. I'm surprised his sweat didn't run green with it. Sometimes it was difficult to believe there was any blood tie between us whatsoever. Half-brother? Not even a quarter-brother. It was because of him I'd always avoided having boyfriends – went out of my way not to attract that kind of attention. Hence the no make-up and the long, 'untended' brown hair pulled forward to cover most of my face – making it look even longer and thinner, I suppose. Not going after boys got me called all sorts of names. Especially by other girls. But if Pierre was anything to go by, young males were simply another species and we had nothing to say to each other.

Then I met Driss.

It was early spring.

Pale and delicate blossoms emerging from hard brown wood. New chestnut leaves like neatly pleated skirts of the freshest green. And a small child trying to skip in the sun.

One of the sweetest memories: sitting beside each other under that tree in the Buttes Chaumont, our arms touching from elbow to shoulder, comfortable and familiar with each other's flesh, feeling the hard, ridged bark of the ancient tree at our backs. Sunlight filtered through the new green of late April leaves. We both had exams, reading to do. We'd go ages without saying anything, then he'd say, 'Did you know …?' and tell me something. Then a bit later I'd say, 'I don't get this.' And he'd explain it if he could. The complete peace of being easy with each other, and with ourselves.

Peace.

But it only lasts a moment. The picture of us in the sweet green light hurtles away from me. 'Come back!' I shout inside my head.

But it's sucked back into the past, smaller and smaller – wrong end of the telescope – away, away down the tunnel of time it goes. The word 'irredeemable' collects behind my eyes, and suddenly my cheeks are wet with the lives I didn't live – or just with that one life I so much wanted to live.

Bastard. *BASTARD*.

If only there were some comfort. The sweet green light here makes it worse. The gap between the sweetness of it and the torture of knowing I'm forever bereft of it. No comfort will come to me. What comfort can there be? Only voices.

Voices. Inside me? Outside me? (Whatever.)

Oscar Wilde saying, 'Go to her, Gertie.'

Gertie. Gertrude. Gertrude Stein. In front of me now, hands on hips, solid, authoritative. Just what I need, maybe. Firm but kind. Kindness, above all, is what I want.

Stein saying, 'Now, my poodle, this won't do, won't do at all. Before we can help you, help you in any way that help can be helpful to the way that you are, there must be some knowing going on between the us of us and the you of you, so tell, tell, and in the telling there may be some knowing going between us, so …' (I frown with the concentration: words turning round and round on themselves … eternal return … eternal return …) 'Let me put it to you another way. There is a certain feeling one has in one when some one is not a whole one to one even though one seems to know all the nature of that one. Such a one then is very puzzling and when sometimes such a one is a whole one to one all the repeating coming out of them has meaning as part of a whole one. When someone is not a clear one to one, repeating coming out of them has not this clear relation. Then such a one is puzzling until they come to be a whole one.'

Proust, putting it simply: 'A full confession, Mademoiselle. Friends should tell each other everything, don't you agree?'

His first words to me were, 'Draw me a sheep.' He used to tease me afterwards about how my jaw dropped open but my eyes lit up as if he'd 'spoken the password to my soul'.

I'd gone to a café after school with Marie-Odile to avoid going home: Pierre was bringing some of his friends back after school. I knew them: they were unbearable. Marie-Odile spent as little time as possible at home anyway; it was all big scenes and arguments because her parents' marriage was disintegrating. We were trying to prepare work for a class the next day, but the place was so noisy it was hard to concentrate. Marie-Odile went off to the loo. And suddenly there he was, leaning over from the next table saying, 'Draw me a sheep.'

To my look of dumb surprise, he shrugged and said, 'You look so sad I thought maybe your plane had crashed in the desert a thousand miles from any human habitation.'

The familiar words from the favourite book of my childhood – *Le Petit Prince* – a book I could still recite almost word for word – were, indeed, a password to something, even if not my 'soul'.

I pretended not to be smiling, reached for a white paper napkin someone had left on the table, took my pen and drew a box. I handed it to him very seriously with, 'That's its box. The sheep you want is inside.'

By the time Marie-Odile came back to the table we'd been trading quotes from *Le Petit Prince* for five minutes. Her eyes flicked from him to me a couple of times before she picked up her bag and said, 'I've just remembered there's something I need from the library' – and exited before I had time to say, 'I'll come with you.' What would my life have been if I'd followed her out of the café? One of those irrevocable moments that are utterly decisive but when you don't really seem to make a decision: it seems decided for you. But I deny it was pure contingency. There must've been something in me – in the history of me – that directed my choice to sit there absurdly quoting from Saint-Exupéry with a short young man of two-minutes' acquaintance rather than running after my long-standing female friend. Even if she'd rushed off faster than she actually did, I could've found her at the library: I knew where she'd be. But I chose to stay there with him. I chose.

Didn't I?

I make an heroic effort to look straight into the puzzling green, straight at Stein, Proust, Wilde, Apollinaire. For a moment they merge and I think it's Driss there – a green hologram of him. Such a feeling of … friendship – of being allies. I reach out to touch him … But the hologram divides again – Stein, Proust, Wilde, Apollinaire – and I'm bereft once more, cheated of his wholeness.

Il pleure dans mon cœur …   There is weeping in my heart …

Thoughts rise and swell in a seethe of bubbles. My mouth is big with them. But they refuse to burst into words. They grow and grow inside my head – pushing against the skull. The words are –

The words are –

'What difference does it make if the gun's loaded? One more drop in an ocean of blood. Small ocean – big universe. Doesn't mean *anything* …'

I hear myself say, 'It's all so senseless. I just wanted to get it over.'

Proust is appalled. 'Such a *young* lady and wanting to get life over!'

'I meant death. I wanted to get death over.'

Proust shakes his head, looks attentively at me. '*Chère* Mademoiselle, that is an impossibility. Death, once it comes, we are never done with.'

I watch the girl to see how she reacts to this. Will it make her long for life? Make her struggle to hold on to whatever …

She begins to stand up: Gertrude Stein and Héloïse help to steady her. (Strong women … kind women … like Grandma Robertson, like Driss's mother.)

'I think what I really meant was I wanted to get the dying over with.'

Apollinaire, with his head like a late Roman emperor but swathed in white, looks down at her with an expression of infinite compassion.

His brown hand in my white one – like an old Third-World charity poster, or something to do with the UN.

But it was the voice I wanted so badly.

His voice singing, always a bit out of tune (but it never stopped him trying) …

His voice murmuring silly endearments: 'You're the soup that warms my stomach.' (What!!). 'Your kneecaps are nearly as amazing as your big toe – the left one …'

His preaching voice. Trying to sound like his father? – or really sounding like him? (I was never sure.) 'We all have to work at our humanity.'

His angry voice. 'Why? WHY? *WHY?*' – his hand slapping the newspaper: some new outrage – his eyes blazing.

His laughing voice – and the laughter itself.

His voice whining, irritating, when he had a 'really, really, really BORING essay' to write, or a 'really, really – you've no idea – BORING book' to read. ('Just do it, Driss. Fussing makes it worse.' 'But you don't understand how …' 'Yes I do. Now just shut up and do it. I've got to finish this …')

His voice respectful and gentle to the schizophrenic girl who slept in a doorway on his parents' street. 'Mademoiselle … *excusez-moi*, Mademoiselle – my mother sent you this. She's made too much food again. She keeps forgetting my brother doesn't live with us any more. She hates to throw food away. Would you accept it – to please her, Mademoiselle?'

If I'd even had a recording of his voice, then maybe …

'Mademoiselle! Mademoiselle!'

I'm annoyed with the voice. It isn't *his* voice. I squint through the green light to see where it's coming from.

'Mademoiselle! Mademoiselle!'

Proust is trying to call the girl back from her memories. Bitterness is collecting in her eyes, constricting her throat. The light turns a poisonous, arsenic green.

'Mademois …'

'Don't keep calling me "Mademoiselle",' she snaps. 'It sounds stupid.' (She's spitting putrid green.) 'Call me Zade, if you have to call me anything. Zade.'

The day he worked his magic, turned me from a threadbare girl everyone called 'Nobi' into Zade – transforming the silliness of my polysyllabic names into something that was simple and exotic at the same time. A lovely neat tapestry woven from the long threads of other names. Zenobia Aurélia Delphine Eugénie: Zade. Energetic but dignified, he said.

'Call me Zade.'

Silence.

'Just call me Zade … please.'

She's calm again. A peaceful green silence.

The word 'b – e – n – e – d – i – c – t – i – o – n' forms in the soft green air, the letters round and gentle and very, very still.

Completely quiet.

Quiet.

When sound begins again it's as a gentle humming, a melody – though scarcely a melody – just a shaping of the moment into music: something between the 'Humming Chorus' from *Madame Butterfly* and a chanted Kaddish.

When the half-heard music fades, there's another moment of absolute and blessed silence … before Oscar breaks it with a cheerful, 'What a curious name! Zade. Sounds somewhat oriental. Or is it short for something?'

'Zenobia Aurélia Delphine Eugénie. After a grandmother and three old aunts I never knew.'

Oscar gives a little cough. 'Some parents are *inordinately* cruel to their children. I think I'd go for the acronym, too, in your position. Wouldn't have worked for me – Oscar Fingal O'Flahertie Wills. Ghastly mouthful. And anyway, as one becomes famous, one can simply shed names – like a balloonist, rising higher, shedding unnecessary ballast. My ambition was to get down to just one and be known simply as 'the Oscar' or 'the Wilde'. And then, of course, once I was *infamous*, I changed my name completely for a bit: Sebastian Melmoth. Silly name – deliberate, of course. It was after that terrible business of Bosie. Dearest, *dearest* Bosie … You're not the only star-cross'd lover, you know, young lady. Not by a long shot. Oh no, not by a …'

And Oscar's words explode into a heart-rending vision of all the star-cross'd lovers that lodge in my brain, a harrowing procession led by Romeo and Juliet –

(From forth the fatal loins of these two foes
A pair of star-cross'd lovers ...)

– a mournful vision of people with yearning, tear-brimmed eyes and outstretched, empty arms, men and women dressed in every age there's been –

(O I am fortune's fool!)

– me on the end of that cruel carnival.

(For never was a story of more woe
Than this of Juliet and her ...)

'At least,' I hear Gertrude Stein whisper to Proust, 'while Oscar keeps talking, the talking is taking her mind off the gun.'

Suddenly the distance between the girl and myself is growing more quickly. Part of me wants this greater separation, the calm, wry distance of it – to go further and further away ... Part of me longs to be back in the turmoil of a life being lived – even if it's a death being endured.

It's a feeling I recognise, this splitting, this sense of being outside the self, watching the self. The first time it happened I was fifteen. A dull February afternoon. Coming home from the *lycée* in a grey light. A sense of meaninglessness. Looking at myself from the outside. 'Who's that pathetic creature down there?'

Just hormones? Maybe all 'existential anguish' is body chemistry. A chemistry that determines we will die. Rot away. Unless efficiently burnt first.

Isn't it excusable to feel anguish at this?

Nature's trap, maybe. A sense of finiteness, infinitesimalness, dawns on you just as the body becomes able to reproduce, offering a way out of total annihilation. Anguish as part of natural selection. Without it, the species might falter.

Then what am I doing with a gun, on my own in a cemetery in the middle of the night when thousands of young women all over the city are moving their bodies with that instinct for creation, their men inside them, working for pleasure? Ruckled sheets, the sharing of moisture and smells, primitive undulations of sea-creatures and the fish-smell of semen confirming our beginning in oceans, millennia on millennia of couplings driving forward, forward through time, a blind force thrusting in the dark …

So if it's only *that* – survival, procreation, evolution, passing on the genes – why aren't I on the other side of these walls in some room, on my back, with the weight of a man on my long, light bones, the hair of his body strange on the smooth pallor of my flesh?

If it's all just survival, evolution, the gene pool, why does it matter so much that it wouldn't be *him* moving on me, moving in me?

Why didn't it work with Lucien?

I tried an experiment. I took Lucien to the same tree I'd sat under with Driss that time, thinking it might be possible to recapture – to create again – something of that feeling. I bought him a book I thought he'd enjoy. It was a later time of year, so the light wasn't quite the same – the leaves were darker, thicker by then. I tried to work it so we sat with our arms touching from elbow to shoulder. But he kept wanting to put his arm around me, or pawing me. He wasn't interested in the book and I couldn't say to him, 'I just want you to sit there with the top of your arm touching mine – you reading and telling me things from time to time and us looking at the light together.' He'd have known I was really after something that wasn't anything to do with him.

The utter irreplaceability of one person by another.

It was the last time I tried turning him into Driss. I just ended up making myself so sad. That dull green light …

An old green blanket of sadness wraps itself around me, hangs limp from my shoulders. A hard and itchy blanket: all weight and no warmth.

I have a right to be sad. I'm a character from Beckett, drooping there in an old blanket, my long, haunted face, my Giacometti legs, shuffling about in a rot-green light. It comes to us all … comes to us all …

Nothing to be done.

And all so silly.

Silly seeing everything in green. Absurd. It brings a kind of laughter to the throat. A singing type of laughter like the sounds in the throats of starlings in a summer tree. The garden of the Normandy house … Stop it. Forget all that.

The laughter in the throat.

Laughter. I can feel it, convulsive, trying to get out.

Getting the giggles in church – silly old men chanting off-key and not even realizing. Madeleine nudging me, my head hanging, shoulders shaking with the effort of stifling the laughter because it was all so silly – touching but silly – all that God the Father stuff and men thinking they've got a special message from God to say only they can be priests. I refused to go after that. 'Teenage rebellion', Madeleine called it, and thought it was just to spite her. My father was more gentle about it and used to stay home with me some Sunday mornings. I think he was glad of the excuse. I never really believed in his 'belief'. He just went for a quiet life because Madeleine went on and on about things. On those Sunday mornings together, the apartment was very quiet. We would read, and sometimes he'd ask me to play my flute to him. He knew how Pierre used to make it hard for me to practise. As Pierre remained singularly 'un-Christian', despite weekly Mass – and Madeleine too, for that matter, showed very few of the Christian virtues (she was vain, selfish, domineering) – I was confirmed in my judgement that the whole thing was absurd.

Absurd. It became my favourite word for a while. I would see ridiculousness in something, and the laughter would start to bubble up, convulsing my throat …

Absurd, seeing everything in green. Absurd, this bizarre tragicomedy being played out in my head. Is it dreaming? If it's death, it's not what I'd expected at all. Lurid but touching; silly, yet profound.

The six letters 'a – b – s – u – r – d' hang over the scene on a banner flapping loose in a careless breeze.

I'm staring at a gabbling playwright, trying to hang on to something, trying to grasp the significance of something that keeps slipping away … slipping away … between the words rising from Oscar Wilde's mouth. Thoughts from a cartoon head … Bubbles from a goldfish …

Finally I manage to concentrate. He's asking me a question.

'And may one inquire as to your surname?'

'Robertson-Bec,' I answer, flatly, as to some uniformed official.

'Now, that's not French.'

'Robertson's English – I'm half and half.'

'French and English you say… But, dear young lady, which half is which? I hope to God the brain is French.'

'And what's wrong with having an English one?' (Despite what he did, she leaps to the defence of her English father and of her grandmother with the smiling blue eyes.)

'Oh, the English mind! – always in a rage. The race wastes its intellect on the sordid and stupid quarrels of second-rate politicians and third-rate theologians – and it's quite *dominated* by the fanatic.' (I realize he's quoting himself. Is that the horror of death, then? Never being able to add anything new to what you've said in life? Known by the words you've said. Having them said again in different contexts being the most one can hope for? The infinite repetition of eternity. Eternal return. Oscar Wilde quoting Oscar Wilde, over and over …) 'England's ideals are *emotional*, not intellectual. What's more, your typical Englishman is always dull and usually violent.'

'And I suppose the French *aren't*. What was that they did in Algeria: fucking *party* games?'

Even I am slightly taken aback by her sudden and crude lashing out at poor, amiable Oscar.

'*Algeria*, dear young lady?'

'Yes, *Algeria*! But I suppose that was after your time. Things weren't so *abominable* back then.'

In the tense silence, Wilde's face drains of all humour. The green air begins to darken. The distance grows between us. I'm embarrassed for her. Has she really fallen into that banal trap of idealizing the past? 'Golden Age'. 'Arcadia'. All that stuff? Or is this the way she protects herself against the despair of the present?

'Get yourself some proper history lessons. You know nothing ... *nothing* ...' Oscar's dark tone is matched by the changing light – bluish-green, becoming bluer by the second.

A voice in my head hisses and sizzles with more of Oscar's words: '*Silently we went round and round ... Silently we went round and round ... Silently we went ...*' I try to shake the sound of the prison-yard picture out of my mind and back into the black-bound book from my father's shelf with its inscription to my English grandfather's name from someone called Jonathan, Xmas, Oxford, and a year long ago. The book's open, there in my head, but the words won't jump back on to the pages – and more begin to sneak out to hiss in my ears – '*sweet things changed to bitterness*' ... '*out of his mouth a red red rose ... out of his mouth a red red rose ...*' I feel the roots of it groping down my throat.

A sound like a dry sob stifles my voice, cuts off my own *De Profundis*. '*Out of the depths have I cried to thee ...*' turns to '*out of his mouth a red red rose ...*'

Then the girl waves the gun at them all – a grand gesture of dismissal (hopelessly melodramatic) and rushes off into the murky blue as if into her own inner darkness.

('*O dark dark dark ... all go into the dark ...*')

I lose sight of her. Part of me is quite happy to let her go, her and her anger. The lonely dark's where they belong. But part of me wants to follow her. Or send a good friend after her. What kind of friend does she need? Someone of passionate intelligence … (I had a friend once, whose passionate intelligence … He was everything to me – everything …) Someone like …

Héloïse is striding off after the girl, full of concern, rosary rattling – with Abelard in determined pursuit.

Find her. Find her. Bring her out of the dark.

… seven … eight … nine … ten. Coming! Hide and seek. Crouched in the corner of the English shed in Grandma Robertson's garden. The smell of old earth and creosote and the musty stifle of the sack I'd pulled over myself, not wanting to be found – ever – because I'd been rude to horrible Auntie Ellen, who would probably tell Grandma.

Find her!

Oscar is reassuring. 'Don't worry, she won't get far – not in those big boots.'

Apollinaire's more urgent, on edge. 'We must stay with her or she may give up completely.'

'Come on, then, let's hurry,' says Oscar. 'We'll form a search-party and go the opposite way to Héloïse and Abelard. Gertrude – you stay here in case she comes back …'

Proust raises his hand as if with an offer of help.

'No, Marcel. We need to hurry and you'll just have an asthma attack. If she comes back, resort to anything to keep her. Tell her your story, if necessary. Get her searching for lost time or something.'

They disappear into the dark.

The voice of Gertrude Stein murmuring, 'I hope to God they find her in time … in time … in time …'

Tick. Tock. Tick. Tock.

Dandelion clock … one o'clock, two o'clock, three o'clock, four … 'What's the time, Mister Wolf?' Playing with the English cousins. The house in Surrey. Grandfather clock. Not far from London. Big Ben. The photo crooked to get in the clock on the top. Me in my new English scarf. Smiling? Smiling.

In search of lost time.

Will they find her in time? – or out of time? Dead or alive. Wanted.

Tick. Tock. Tick. Tock. Tick. –

'If time is space and space is time …'

I'm on my back, stark naked under the night sky. Smell of strawberries and sandalwood.

A sweltering July night. We've heaved ourselves up through the skylight (still clothed), along with a duvet to lie on, a bowl of strawberries, a carton of milk, two glasses and a sandalwood joss-stick. Driss had discovered a small area of flat roof we could get to. Our usual room was stifling.

They thought I'd gone to the country for the weekend with Marie-Odile's family. It'd been a legitimate arrangement, but I made my excuses to her mother at the last moment. Risky – but worth it.

We spread the blue duvet and put the white bowl of strawberries in the middle. The heat brought out their sweet smell: they didn't need sugaring.

I poured two glasses of milk while Driss lit the joss-stick.

'What's that for?'

'The air stinks of traffic fumes, even up here. It's the heat.'

I took the softest-looking strawberry and it collapsed on to the light-blue shift I was wearing – the coolest thing I could find. I tried to pick it up, but a bit more fell off. Two pinky-red stains in my lap.

When the strawberries and milk were finished and the sandalwood was drifting well over our roof-space, Driss said, 'Take your clothes off.'

'Well, there's nothing like being direct!' I laughed.

'No – I don't mean for sex. I just mean take your clothes off – all of them.' He was already removing his. And no – not a hint of arousal.

'Strawberries obviously don't do it for you. Or was it the milk?'

'It's too hot for sex.'

'Then why do we need to strip?'

'Trust me.'

'Why should I?'

'Because you love me.'

'Smug bastard.'

We lay down, side by side, stone-still, like Héloïse and Abelard on their tomb – but naked. Just the tips of our fingers touching.

'Close your eyes.'

'What are you going to do?'

'An experiment. Close your eyes. Tight. I'm doing it, too. Then after I've counted to five, open them very wide, looking straight up, and don't blink, and don't say a word for as long as you can bear it. Okay? Are they closed? Right. One – two – three – four …'

It was dreadful.

It was marvellous.

It was the death of oneself and it was a sharper awareness

of 'self' than I'd ever known. Beneath the vast blackness, my maggot-coloured body with its hair sprouting in peculiar places. I was no longer 'me' at all. I was just a biological system, gene-driven, DNA moulded, a representative of the species, a clump of cells, a 'bare forked animal'. Nothing between the white skin of my belly and the nearest star.

While the great silent nothingness pressed down from above, beneath you could hear the city, all energy and fizz, all squabbles and laughter through the open windows of the hot and sleepless night. A saxophone somewhere. The throb of rock music from somewhere else. Traffic. A siren. All the tangle and fidget and edginess of humans trying to live together in a big city –

The city rising up beneath me, the universe forcing itself down on me from above. Small and naked, sandwiched between the two.

I took his hand, held on tight to stop myself disappearing altogether. His hand was the only thing that made me feel 'there'.

I woke to the throaty little sound of a pigeon near my head and a chilly, whitish-grey light. The pigeon was picking among the small green stars of strawberry stalks that had been in a neat pile. It twitched them, tossed them about, grumbling in its chest. The joss-stick was a little heap of ash. The glasses were dulled with the residue of milk. A corner of the duvet was over my legs and hips. Driss was curled against me –

– wearing my dress!

I laughed, startling the pigeon. It flapped clumsily off. Driss opened one eye.

'What are you doing in my dress?!'

'What?'

'My dress. You're wearing it.'

'Mmmm … I was cold.' Slurred, sleepy words.

'I'm cold. I need it.'

Both his eyes were shut again, but he reached beneath his head where his rolled-up black T-shirt had been a pillow. He pushed it in my direction and returned to his original curled-up position.

'Driss. DRISS …'

I gave up and put on his T-shirt, lay down again and tried to pull more of the duvet over me.

He put his arms around me. He was more awake than he'd let on.

I made love to a man in a blue dress.

I'm cold. So cold. Blue with cold. (What did I expect?) Marble cold.

I don't want to be cold, don't want to be laid on a slab in the dark. Where *is* she? If only I hadn't let her go off like that, alone into the annihilating dark. Part of me despises her for bolting. Part of me loves her still, wants her to go on trying, struggling …

My love has turned into friends running after her, searching for her so she's not swallowed by the dark, unable to find her way back. There goes Oscar Wilde. There goes Apollinaire. There's Proust and Stein, waiting, hoping. Héloïse and Abelard believe they're on her trail.

But perhaps I'll never see her again. I'm being drawn away and upwards – rising, rising above the cemetery – higher and higher – more and more detached from the earth, suspended above the city. Up … up …

A restless wind begins to blow around me. It tugs and pulls me through the spaces of the dark, and it shakes the memory – a madman shaking a dead chrysanthemum.

Flowers for the dead. All Saints. The yearly visit to her grave. My father's big hand holding mine. Madeleine silent, seething, on our return, because he insisted on going, year after year. I remember it as always windy. Hair in my mouth, scarf unwrapped by it. And always a pot of chrysanthemums – allowing me to choose the colour. The pink or white turned to purple and then dark bronze as I grew out of childhood's colours. The journey out of Paris to the suburban cemetery near where she'd grown up. And always the wind around my ankles and head.

Driss was afraid of the wind. Perhaps not afraid, exactly, just rather jittery when it blew too hard. He'd been caught in a storm once, on a childhood holiday – literally blown off his feet by the violence of it. He said the worst thing wasn't the grazed knees and the bruised elbow – it was the feeling of being utterly helpless in the face of a power you couldn't control and that was totally physical, totally without mind.

I now know there are people like that. Which is even more frightening.

Rising up and up above it all, I feel a great wind pulling me through the restless dark.

... *vent mauvais*	... evil wind
Qui m'emporte	which takes me
Deçà, delà	here, takes me there
Pareil à la	as if I'm a
Feuille morte.	fallen leaf.

Like a Chagall figure, I'm flying, horizontal, suspended above all human habitation. The wind I feel on my face pulls back my hair and draws the clouds back from the moon, unveiling her widow's face with its washed-out, blotchy look: her light gives an eerie tinge to the deeply night-time blue. And the same wind sweeps in fitful gusts through the streets down there. Tin cans are bowled along by it, as if kicked by ghosts. Cats are startled, on edge. Leaves and grimy scraps of paper are lifted and swept along by invisible brooms; they collect in corners. Late walkers have their hair grabbed and tousled; they pull up collars, plunge hands in pockets, sink chins into coats against the sudden chill. Manic little vehicles with their mindless sounds, darting about even at this hour. A jumble of buildings with chattering signs, still winking at the eyeless night.

That life down there, it looks so odd. Who'd want it? – its fidgety day-to-dayness, its piece of apple skin stuck between the teeth, smells from the body – cleaning it, cleaning it – and the nuisance of hair and feeding and clearing up after feeding, and being irritated by a woman with too-orange powder on her face and by the squeaky voice of a concierge who means well and is cross-eyed (the itch of guilt). That life of continual testing and examinations and blame for things not done, not achieved, and all the things you don't know, can't know – like the truth about anything, *anything*, and people with silly beliefs that ruin other people's lives, and the hungry and the dispossessed and feeling so helpless in the face of it all – and the violence, the howling hysteria of violence. Hopeless mother over her dead child. (Every Pietà, living Guernicas). The child over her dead mother (solemn procession of chrysanthemums, measuring out the years with them). And a lover who …

Perhaps I should leave Zade down there, in the cemetery. It might be kinder. It would be the easiest thing in the world to continue rising … way, way above the whole city … up, up, further and further into the blue and silver coldness that has nothing more to do with the sweating earth, with what is human. It would be so easy … skylark easy …

But what would I lose up there in the icy realms of not-being? What would I miss? What would make the infinite effort of hanging on worthwhile?

Like opening Grandma Robertson's button-box, I lift the lid to a bizarre mixture – from humble little shirt buttons to those in the shape of flowers made from forget-me-not glass …

Music – that Poulenc piece I played for my last flute exam, all spirit and energy and delicious intervals between the notes … The Bach cello suites, of course. Some silly old songs, touching songs – my father's old record of Serge Gainsbourg singing *Le Poinçonneur des Lilas* ('*Des petits trous, des petits trous …*' No, don't think of that now, it's too sad …) …

That old paperback of Verlaine, second-hand and inscribed to Clothilde from Jean-Pierre with many kisses (Are they still together, whoever they were?) – the yellow cover with the spine sun-faded to primrose, on the front 'Verlaine' in red, a blue panel with a black drawing of three people going into a café … and always falling open at page eighteen. I knew it by heart –

La lune blanche	The white moon
Luit dans le bois;	Shines in the wood;
De chaque branche	From each branch
Part une voix	A voice slips away
Sous la ramée …	Beneath the leaves …

O bien aimée.	O well-beloved.
L'étang reflète,	The pool – deep mirror –
Profond miroir,	Reflects
La silhouette	The silhouette
Du saule noir	Of the black willow
Où le vent pleure …	Where the wind weeps …
Un vaste et tendre	A vast and tender
Apaisement	Quietening
Semble descendre	Seems to descend …

No! Don't go on with that. I don't want a 'vast and tender quietening'. I want something to give me the will to go back down there. I want to go back. Want to go back. Even if it'll all be so hard – love, hate, passion, recriminations.

I want to go back, even to the continual battle with ideas, and just trying to keep up with day-to-day life – anything, but not this silver-cold detachment. Not this! That girl doesn't know what she's doing, choosing to go off into the dark like that. Where is she? WHERE IS SHE?

I will myself back to the island of the dead.

There it is – down there. Père Lachaise –

The wind's grabbing petals from yesterday's chrysanthemums, pulling at fading silk and plastic; it plays with the half-bare trees along the grid of avenues – the moon shadows the branches into moving black patterns across a silvered path between the tombs … and across a figure –

A travers les branches du temps	Through the branches of time
J'ai regardé passer ton ombre …	I watched your shade pass …

– two figures – a man and a woman – hurrying along it. Flowing garments play and flap around their limbs as they stride through the windy blue dark.

I strain my ears for the human sounds I want so much to hear. Have they found her?

The man is panting – can scarcely keep up with the woman. Then, through his deathbed rasp of breath, I hear a speaking voice once more.

I smile when I realize who they are. Theirs is a story I know so well. And the first time I read it I wept and wept – for her, for him, for the love, the passion, the cruelty of it all, when we only have one life, one chance. Their story leaps to new life in my head. (More star-cross'd lovers?) There they are, on the path in the dark.

To smile or to grieve now as I watch them? I'm not sure which it deserves.

Love. Do we take it with us? Will what we mean to each other go on for aeons, but in a time that's out of Time, the single moment of eternity in an absolute 'now'? And if we take the love with us into that moment that lasts for ever, do we also take the doubts, the bickering, the falling out, the reconciliations? Purged of passion? – or tortured still by the underside of love, the insidious voices of jealousy, uncertainty, disappointment, fear of losing it?

'Héloïse! … Slow down … Have a care … for my age … and condition …'

The robed woman strides on muttering, 'I'll have as much care as *you* had for my youth and vulnerability.'

'What did … you say? …'

'Oh, nothing.' She sighs, irritated, but waits for him to catch up, freeing her face from the blue cloth veil the wind has whipped across it. Her mouth unmuffled again, she calls, 'You don't have to be part of this.'

'I don't like you going about on your own.'

'Still "protective", Peter? – or should the adjective be "possessive"?'

He grabs her arm and holds it tight, bringing his blue face close to hers – two proud and handsome profiles sculpted in moonlight.

'It was for our own protection – especially for *yours* – that I insisted on Holy Orders.'

'*You* insisted – exactly. Deposit me in a convent, then don't bother to write, visit or anything. You had what you wanted, and when you couldn't have *that* any more' (she glances to where a certain part of his anatomy is missing), 'you wanted to make sure I didn't either.'

He slaps her face.

She slaps him back – then pulls away and hurries on, her head held high. (Is her cheek stinging? Are there tears in her eyes?)

'It was your mind I was in love with!' he shouts after her, his voice half drowned by the howling wind.

'Driss, why do you love me?'

'It's your ears – they're so neat. And the way your shoulder-blades look when you stretch. And those little round bones on the outer sides of your wrists. And your brain. I love your brain.'

'Aren't you supposed to like the sexy bits of me?'

'The mind, also, is an erogenous zone …' He plunged his hands into my hair and explored my skull with his fingertips. 'Oh, man … just feel those bumps …' He started covering my head with kisses, then pushed me back on to the bed. 'Sorry. Can't control myself when I feel those bumps …' – until I was laughing so much he put his hand over my mouth (the walls were thin) … and we made love again.

'My mind! Don't you dare start on that again,' she calls over her shoulder, turning off the path and passing with agile steps between the close-packed tombs. 'You'd never have wanted me if I'd been a hunchback, no matter how clever I was.'

'Héloïse … Héloïse …' He keeps stumbling on the irregular steps and plinths around the graves. Dead leaves are whisked into life around the hem of his blue robe. 'Don't let's argue again, my dear sister in Christ.'

'Sister in Christ! *Sister in Christ!*' she shouts. 'We're man and wife, for God's sake. We're *parents*.' She reduces her voice to a vigorous whisper that's woven with the wind. 'How do you think I felt about your sister bringing up Astralabe? *Our child* dumped with your *provincial* family and …'

The plans we had for our children! Such wonderful people we'd make of them – loving and kind and knowing so much and all their talents given the chance to develop and confident and not afraid to speak out but watchful that their words wouldn't hurt. Such people that angels would have felt inadequate before them … I was going to make sure my family had as little to do with them as possible.

We'd try to imagine what they'd look like. They'd be small, of course. Of the three requirements of the 'ideal man', Driss only met one – dark. He had a nice face, but not what most people would call handsome. And he certainly wasn't tall. We

51

were exactly the same height. Our children stood little chance of looking 'distinguished', given two such ordinary little parents. But we'd give them big spirits – spirits that were *huge* – to make up for their small bodies. They were going to be the most loved and loving children in the whole world. They were going to be …

'How was I to know what you felt about my family bringing him up? You never mentioned it in your letters.'

'Do you have *no* imagination, Peter? Has *everything* got to be written down before it means anything to you? Just another obtuse male, despite your famous cleverness.'

'He was my son, too. I loved him.' (The wind whines on through the blue-black branches and the staring stones.)

'Oh, yes – "the poem". Advice to your son. Worst thing you ever wrote. Huh! Let's face it, my Uncle Fulbert was probably right. You just wanted to ditch your responsibilities to me and the child and get on with your work – your big, important work.'

'But *you* wanted me to as well. *You* could see the Church needed an injection of reason. I had to try. I *had* to. And if your vicious uncle hadn't …'

'I warned you it wouldn't work – that he'd never agree to keep the marriage secret. And you only wanted it that way so it wouldn't interfere with your career plans. Married clergy couldn't get as far up the ladder, could they?'

'If you ask me, your Uncle "Castrator" Fulbert had designs on you himself. But I came along just a bit too soon – so he took his revenge on me by …'

'I never wanted to marry you, anyway. I was happy to be your mistress. It was your body I loved and I'm not afraid to admit it. And I never did care a toss for "respectability". My education and

my brains freed me from *that* little trap. What's more … Sshhh!'
She suddenly ducks behind a large blue headstone, beckoning
Abelard to do the same. 'I think I hear something.'

He obeys, creeps up behind her and they both kneel behind the
same stone. They listen for a few moments, very close. Nothing.
(Even the wind is lulling to a breeze now.) Then, tentatively, as
if half expecting another slapped cheek, he places an arm around
her. He finds her irresistible still. She allows the arm to remain.
He whispers, 'Héloïse, my dearest, forgive me – yet again.'

I watch her turn slowly towards him. The wind has dropped.
In the bright blue moonlight, his eyes glitter strangely.

Kneeling, breast to breast now, they clasp each other – two
book-ends with no books between them.

It's over. They've played out their little scene and it twists my
heart. Is this their eternity? Infinite repetition?

So what would mine be? – an infinite repetition of …

I want to be with the girl again, want to shrink the distance
between us. To warn her. Eternity … You simply take your life
with you.

Or is it too late for warnings?

Dead?

Dying?

Or dreaming of death?

The canopied tomb of Héloïse and Abelard. There they are, supine, chastely parallel, returned to moonlit stone. What dreams define their eternity? Did they even know the world was round? Beneath their stones, the dreams of the dead locked in the world as they knew it, the universe as they conceived of it. The worst thing about death, perhaps – never to see the world move on. Dreams of the plague still raging across Europe … Side by side, the dead down the ages dream of Napoleon or Auschwitz, mazurkas or jazz. Underground it doesn't much matter, perhaps – the pictures whirling, settling like snow in the skull. But among the living locked in different worlds in their heads, bound up in different dreams from different realities – and trying to live side by side in the same world, the same cities. And it's not simply *difference* – it's when one 'reality' impinges on another, refuses to accept it, refuses the different realities. Like believing in heavenly rewards for … God on our side – all that. What happened to my mother …

No. That's the last thing I need to think of now. I want the comfort of love, not to be reminded of …

I want the comfort of friends.

My need brings me back to them – brings *them* back to *me*. Two of them right there – Stein and Proust, sitting together on a flat grave and luminous in silver-blue light, patient, as if hoping the girl will come back to them. I love them: they're part of me. ('You are what you read.' Madame Seignette's mantra – every lesson …) Can they love me?

The odd one. The loner. The virgin. The dyke. The sullen one. The quiet one. Always reading. The boring one. Me.

If, instead of sticking labels on me, those who thought they knew me had looked inside the box, they'd have been blown off their feet by the roar of a bloody revolution thundering on inside me – a revolution against the oppression of boredom and conformity.

Definition of boredom? Being dragged round endlessly to relatives and parents' friends – endless meals, endless talk of nothing that got anybody anywhere. Being told to put on make-up, what to wear, and Madeleine saying, 'For God's sake, can't you try to sparkle a little? The Roussels will think …', and Papa saying, 'Let her be herself, Madeleine.' It was like Musset's story of the white blackbird – one parent saying 'What a nasty child,' the other defending it: 'Can't you see it's just her age?' – though it was the other way round in my life: my father defending me. He used to take my side – as much as he dared. I read his subtext as, 'She's like her mother – her *real* mother.'

My father, a chemist with a big drugs company, weighed words carefully, as if they were substances which, put together in the wrong combination, could have disastrous effects. Ironic, really, in the light of …

Sometimes I wished he'd been less 'balanced' – wished he'd gone mad with grief when his young wife was killed. But perhaps his apparently impassive 'going on', his taking a new wife so different from my mother (I assumed), was a kind of madness: 'might as well do that as anything else'. Like holding a gun to your head and pulling the trigger without knowing whether or not it's loaded. Perhaps I'm more like my father than I thought. At least he never said he did it for me – married again to give me a mother. I wasn't made to feel responsible.

My friendship with Proust began with the business over the mother – that part where Marcel describes longing for his mother to leave her guests and come upstairs to kiss him goodnight. Longing and longing. It tugged at me so strongly because of the ridiculous fantasy that my mother would return, that it'd all been a terrible mistake; she wasn't dead at all. She'd been in a coma. The woman who'd died was someone else. The hospital had got them mixed up. She'd recovered but lost her memory for a long time – had gone in search of her past, her reality, and had finally found it, come back to us; and my father would tell her to stay beside me, just as little Marcel's father had so unexpectedly done … To stay beside me and make up for all the time we'd lost …

I thought my mother must've been something like Marcel's: very loving, yet capable of putting her adult life first when the occasion required it. That's why she'd gone back to work so soon after having me. She was personal assistant to some bigshot at UNESCO. She'd loved her job, my father said. I imagine her quiet, efficient, well-informed, utterly reliable. Her sister – Aunt Clarice – lived not far from us and, as she'd given up her job to look after her two young children, I was added to the household during the day. It was a good arrangement. Aunt Clarice's husband earned only a modest salary. Life's expensive in Paris. My mother paid her sister for childcare and had the security of knowing I was being cared for in exactly the way she would wish.

I was brought up to believe she'd died in a car crash.

I was three when my father married Madeleine, and Pierre was born soon after.

We never did like each other, even as children, despite our father's exemplary efforts to reconcile us, to be seen to be treating us equally, to make the foursome work as a family unit, and so on. But the only solution was division: Pierre would 'belong' to Madeleine, I to my – our – father. He would take my part (mainly), she his. An uneasy but mainly workable truce. It functioned well enough.

Until I fell in love.

Not even Proust prepared me for that.

I hear a sigh. The wind? No. It's Proust whispering to Stein his stories of lovers. I try to listen from a distance – but his voice seems soft with secrecy.

What *were* his stories? They're slipping away from me. My memory's suddenly smudging as if I'm drifting away from all that, drifting away on a dark sea. It's lonely. Alone with no stories. Out on a dark sea. Drifting away …

No! Not yet! I want to stay with them. Come on – paddle for the shore. Make an effort. Focus. Remember. *Remember*.

That's it!

The return of memory, quite suddenly, with the word 'remember'.

A madeleine. A cup of lime-flower tea. That's how I first met him – Proust – at school. The famous passage about the return of memory. And we had to study one or two other fragments, too … Then there was …

… the chapter on him in my *History of Literature*, and the lovely boxed set of *In Search of Lost Time* from my father that Christmas. It crossed my mind that he might have regretted marrying Madeleine (irritating and meaningless coincidence of her name with the Proustian cake – though I sometimes wished I could've plunged her into scalding liquid) – I imagined how he himself longed to retrieve the past … All very poignant and the kind of thing that appeals to adolescent sentiments.

I didn't understand half of what Proust was really on about: I was too young. But the details – the 'actuality' of lived life, of plants, clothes, people, conversations … It seemed a miracle that anyone could conjure up such realities with words. And it gave me another world to inhabit. As I read and read, that world became more vivid and believable than the world around me – the claustrophobia of family life in our apartment, the daily doses of school and homework … People thought I'd become even more quiet and boring than usual. But they didn't know who my friends were …

Friends. What I long for now, more than anything. It's bitter-sweet to watch two people easy with each other. Bitter-sweet to see, conjured there, Proust and Stein sitting side by side on a flat tombstone. Proust is blue, Stein is blue, matching holograms shaped from moony-blue light, Stein the little less substantial of the two: I don't know her so well. I'd never bothered to read the bit on her in the *History of Literature*. It was Driss who introduced me to her.

At the Musée Picasso, smiling at the blue woman dancing naked in *La Joie de Vivre*. Driss said that, for some reason, the 'spirit' of the painting made him think of Gertrude Stein – though that wasn't surprising, he'd said, because they were friends and all 'that lot' knew how to be serious about playing.

It was something Driss was very good at. Playing. His friends called him 'the joker'. But they didn't realize how serious his jokes really were.

After the Musée Picasso, I went home and spent the evening reading up about Gertrude Stein. I wanted to impress him. She sounded interesting, and because she was writing in Paris at the same time as Proust, I thought maybe their writing was a bit similar. But when I got some of her work out of the library, I found it very hard to understand – even though my English was pretty good. Better than Driss's.

'Okay, boy genius – explain it to me.' I challenged him with a piece from a work called *Tender Buttons*. 'What does it mean?'

'I haven't the faintest idea.'

'But you said you like her!'

'Did I? Yes, I do. I like the idea of her, even if I don't understand her.'

'That's daft.'

'No it isn't. I don't always understand you, but I still like you.' He put on the silly smile he knew made me furious.

'Oh, *you!*' I started to pummel him with ineffectual fists.

He grabbed me, wrestled me on to the sofa and kissed me into submission – as usual.

We were 'light' together – as they are, Proust and Stein, quietly exchanging confidences in the blue of the night.

If only I could have that lightness again – that camaraderie.

We were lovers. We were friends. We were allies. Just to sit and chat together, sharing things we knew, things we'd thought, ambitions, fears … I'm growing darkly envious of these spirits sitting in the moonlight, whispering. Their dialogue seems to grow from jumbles of information in my head.

Proust sighs. 'So, the last of October. Allhallows. Once more the night of restless spirits.'

Stein gives a one-sided smile. 'The penalty of fame. Ironic, isn't it – ironic the way we seek the way of immortality through the art of our art, then, when we find ourselves on the other side of the other side, our continuing life in the continuing world, our shadow-puppet existence, keeps us restless, restlessly dissatisfied. People quarrelling their quarrels over what we meant and mean. Then those who delve and delve in the trash-cans of the emotional lives of our lives for their biographies and essays and parade us in front of a line of fair-ground mirrors and each mirror warps us in a way that is different from the difference of the last. (*"In a little while they smile in a little while and one two three they smile they smile."*)'

'Your last day, Gertrude, do you remember it?'

'Pain, physical pain, and the pain of parting from Alice (*"and always with it a hope is for more not more than yesterday but more today more today more to say more today …"*). The American Hospital in Neuilly. My last words. For some reason I said,

"What is the answer?" and everyone standing around gloomily gloomy and not one of them replying, so I made a big effort to smile and said, "Okay then, what's the question?" I don't think they were quite up to it, my way of coming up to the end. Just the same as always was the same. Couldn't quite keep up with me and my way. Things meaning everything and nothing, nothing and everything. It's all in the *trying* and …'

'Do you miss Alice?'

'Ah – Alice. Miss Alice. (*"We mention many thousands of buds. And when I close my eyes I see them …"*) Alice who didn't like the sun. She comes and goes. She's not entirely not there, but less there than some of us. (*"She is my tender sweet and her little feet are stretched out well which is a treat and very lovely …"*) Her thereness depends on the thereness of me, like a shadow. (*"She is very lovely and mine which is very lovely …"*) But lately, lately, she fades and fades. Sometimes I search – the lover for the beloved, the soul for its mate, and desolation is all, all is desolation of the spirit when love is left but the beloved gone. The word "yearning" has some relevance here …'

(Here the word 'y-e-a-r-n-i-n-g' coils itself above them to the shape of a blue fiddle-head. Poignant music from a violin – then, approaching from a distance, a soprano voice, high notes of a heart-rending aria … *Madame Butterfly* – 'One fine day …' … No, don't think of Butterfly falling on her father's sword. Let the yearning music gentle away to Satie – a piano – the more merciful yearning of a *Gymnopédie* …)

Those weeks when I was utterly in love with every inch of him – but before we'd slept together for the first time. My body woken to adult desire, but alone in its childhood bed every night –

wanting and wanting his body by me, in me. Cuddling my pillow with that urgent excitement in my veins and that yearning throb of unsatisfied desire in the pit of my stomach. Unable to sleep. Hearing, at midnight, the muffled murmurs from the bedroom where my father lay with Madeleine, knowing they had what my body craved, yet finding it odd – unbelievable, almost – that two big and (to me) old bodies might feel the same desperate longing for each other that I felt for Driss's body. No, it must be different for them. No more than the habitual satisfaction of a vague itch, surely – not this utter yearning with the whole of my unsatisfied being. I wrapped my right leg around my left one, trying to convince myself it was his leg, pulling the pillow tighter against my stomach, wanting him so, so much … wanting and wanting …

'And you, Marcel?'

'Some yearning for lovers, yes – for Reynaldo and Alfred especially – but mostly for my mother and my aunt. The problem is they *have* an existence because of my book. But how I created them for that – it's fiction, after all – is not exactly how they were in life. So their afterlife does not coincide precisely with their living selves. Their spirit lives are mainly those conjured by my words in the minds of others, so when I come across *maman* and *ma tante*, I have always a slight sense of … disappointment – a sense of them being other than themselves. Each has become an amalgam of the readings of my book. The word "yearning" reverberates always in my spirit, too.'

'Is that the why of why we're all restless in the afterlife after our life? All amalgams of the way the world has read us. Perhaps that's what we *are* – all of us, everybody. Perhaps there is no self. Perhaps …'

The dialogue fades. Their perhapses rustle into the sound of leaves in a night-time breeze, or waves sighing gently on to an unseen shore, lulling me into a deep, deep sleep, immersing me in a dream more vivid than anything I've yet …

A figure hurtling out of the blue light. Oscar – cape flying, hat gone – calling, 'We've found her … we've found her …'

'Where?'

'By the Communards' Wall.'

'Is she safe?'

'Oh, Gertie, the *poor* girl. They've given her *such* a time of it.'

'Then why have you left her, Oscar, why have …'

'It's all right. Guillaume's nearby for when it's over.'

'Can't you stop them, Monsieur Wilde? Take her away from the place?' urges Proust.

'She has to go through it, has to realize. And there's no comfort, no comfort at all. But she's suffering so much. Pure *anguish*. I can't tell you how …'

I don't wait to hear any more.

I run … run … calling her, calling out my own name into the dark, over and over, calling into the darkness. (*'O dark dark dark. They all go into the dark …'*) Running and calling, and the faster I run the more I'm anchored to the same place, though I feel I'm going deeper into it, as if it's my own mind I'm running through.

(*'… still and still moving
Into another intensity …'*)

It's black ahead, but at the sides of my eyes, in the stream of wind made by my running, as if on the walls of an ill-lit tunnel (ghost-train at the *Foire du Trône*, but no arm around me, no laughing Driss beside me), moving murals of hideous creatures squirm and turn. As I run, they call my own name back to me from mouths hideous with death. I see myself among them – my body, my face – but made up of all the fish I've ever eaten, their dulled eyes staring at me, silvery bodies wrapped and writhing around each other in impossible knots and trying to break free, trying and trying …

It passes.

But now, from niches in the walls of the tunnel I'm running through, gargoyles spit foul words at my head, or laugh and point with clawed little monkey-hands. A pulled-up mandrake screams in a sudden beam of light, and Dali's clocks melt and sob out, '*Redeem the time – Redeem the time –*'.

There's a woman up to her neck in sand but muttering, '*Great mercies … great mercies …*'. Then Picasso's *Woman in Tears* is ripping the air with lurid grief as soldiers march on and on with bandaged-stump feet and eyes melting down blistered cheeks, and one-time musicians have shattered hands and painters are blinded, composers left earless, philosophers out of their minds ('*Where is there an end to it, the soundless wailing …*'), all running now through blasted trees and squelching through corpses, or scrambling up hills of them, skulls crunching under hopeless boots ('*the bone on the beach*') – military boots weary with tramping, turned to Van Gogh boots, Beckett boots – and the skull, the skull – ('*not I, not I*') – on the mountain of shoes, the hill of hair … and pursuing me now, Furies at the sides of my eyes, for ever and ever, the endless swarms of the murdered …

Those who had no choice.

Unlike me. (Stop it.)

Unlike me.

With the hugest of efforts I propel myself forward, out of that tunnel and on to the path that might lead me to *her*.

Where are you? Where *are* you? – you with your big ideas. Hiding behind someone else's tombstone, I suppose. What was it you were going to be? – an artist? – a writer? – a lawyer? Goodness me! – a *lawyer*? Thought you'd put the world to rights, did you? So what are you doing out there in the dark, playing hide and seek? You really want to be found, don't you. It was just a big gesture, wasn't it, running off into the dark, when there didn't seem anything left to do. When it all went wrong. But I'm on my way, silly girl, I'm on my way …

I find her by the Communards' Wall, hitting at it uselessly with her fists – as if it's a tomb closing in around her, suffocating her, and she's desperate for life … life … life … Wave after wave of anguish breaks over her. The only word wrung from her is his name – '*Driss… Driss… Driss …*' It's as if the very word 'anguish' has woven itself together a million times over to make a tight black cloak that wraps and tangles itself around her, keeping her there, by the wall, with only her small fists free to beat at its skin-grazing stones.

Those terrible, terrible days afterwards. Not just the anguish of the mind – trying to take it in – but the body's grief. The terrible, physical longing of the body. It isn't something people talk about. But the grief of the body for its mate is equal to the grief of the mind and emotions for their companion. It's not the kind of thing you're supposed to say. It seems to me people still don't acknowledge their bodies enough – not in the truest, deepest sense …

Driss believed our bodies were all we had. It was the only time we went to Père Lachaise together. We were standing by the Héloïse and Abelard tomb and I came out with some stuff about how lovely it was to think that they were probably happy at last in the afterlife, no more problems, united in love, et cetera, et cetera.

He said, 'You don't really believe that, do you?'

I laughed and said, no, not really.

But I didn't know what I believed, really.

As I watch her hitting the wall my detachment falters because I'm seeing what *she* sees – the swarming presences of the murdered, of those who would have chosen 'life' if they'd had a choice. Victims of anger, revenge, greed, perversion, madness – a six-year-old child, an old woman, Resistance fighters, an old man killed for his wallet, and then, most terrible of all, those endless swarms – men, women, children – that have come to her from the Jewish monuments – Auschwitz, Belsen, Buchenwald, Dachau, Nevengamme – their numberless hands pulling at me for acknowledgment … But 'swarm' suggests anonymity, and their power over me is not as a nameless, featureless mass figured as a few tortured, emaciated figures in those Expressionist monuments haunting that part of the cemetery, but as thousands upon thousands upon thousands of the most sharply defined and tender lives, each unique in its humanity, each with its ambitions, quirks, kindnesses, favourite jokes, memories of the first kiss, a fear of spiders or dentists, a funny-shaped toe on the left foot, loving the smell of apples in a room … not seen as 'millions' but as one upon one upon one upon one upon one upon one upon one …

She can run to the ends of the universe but she'll never rid herself, now, of that knowledge.

Her suffering pulls me back to her. The split is healing. Threads pulling us together again …

The reality of his hand in mine …
The reality of his hand …
The reality …

With a leap of dread I understand why her wish for life is locked in desperate combat with a carelessness about whether to go on living in a world where such barbarity existed, exists … will exist, it seems. I want to help resolve the conflict in her. But I'm too close to her again to know which side I want to fight on, feeling the pull of both. To live. To die. Either seems justifiable.

I turn – and, in the dimness of the indigo light, see a man with a bandaged head approaching me … *Driss?*

No. Too tall.

But it's somebody who's been injured. She thinks it's another dreadful casualty of the world's inhumanity come to torture her.

I, however, still have a sliver of separateness left – enough to recognise him when she doesn't. I try to hold on to her, make her stay: it's only her old friend Apollinaire. But her fear's too strong. She pulls away and runs into indigo night.

This time I won't let her go alone.

All I can do is run with her into the darkness … run and run till the breath rattles in the throat …

He had hold of my hand and started running, looking back over his shoulder with an exaggerated expression of terror. Having no idea what on earth was happening, I ran, looking back from time to time, trying to make out from what or from whom we were running. People stopped, followed the trajectory of Driss's eyes, began to look apprehensive themselves, no doubt in case the person we were running from was armed and mad, in case they were about to get caught up in some pointless massacre. It'd been a fairly quiet shopping street. It turned suddenly quieter as people paused to watch, assess, make ready for fight or flight themselves ... Then the noise rose as questions and confusions found words ... at which point he pulled me into a tiny side street and collapsed in helpless laughter.

'Driss ... what the ... hell's ... going on?' I was breathless, scared, puzzled – and finally angry. It was a joke. Just to see people's reactions.

I told him I thought it was stupid. He said he agreed. He 'didn't know what had come over him'. Sometimes a malicious little Beelzebub climbed inside his skin and made him play a practical joke like that – just to see …

I said I thought it was extremely juvenile of him. He hung his head, said he was sorry, and for the next three hours talked only of Third World poverty, cancer, terrorism, accidents, suicides … until I burst into tears.

'All right,' I sobbed, 'you've made your point.'

A couple of days later, as I approached the cinema where we'd arranged to meet, nearly everybody was looking up into the sky – some still walking along. Two people even bumped into each other as a result. I looked up, too. Nothing.

Driss was already there, head down, earnestly reading a newspaper. I was quick enough to notice his sideways glance: I knew he'd seen me but was pretending he hadn't. With a deliberately casual gesture he turned the page of the newspaper. He pretended I'd made him jump, suddenly appearing beside him like that. But I pinched the skin at the back of his neck hard, held it fast between my thumb and forefinger (the nails of both were long).

'It's you,' I hissed, 'isn't it?'

He blinked innocently behind his glasses. 'Of course it's me. What an odd way to say hello.' But his expression was shifty.

'Look!' I yanked his head up and swivelled it so he had to look at all the people gazing up into an empty sky.

'What's up with you?' he said. 'PMT?'

I shook him by the shoulders. 'You know exactly what I mean. What did you do to make them all start looking up like that?'

He gave a slow exaggerated shrug. 'I was just … standing here, looking up at the sky … thinking what a beautiful summer evening it was. Can't a guy even look up at the sky without being accused by his girlfriend of …?'

'You're impossible!' I stamped my foot with ridiculous theatricality.

'Okay, okay – I'll stop them looking up.' At which point he grabbed me, clamped me in a vice-like embrace, kissed me hard on the mouth so I could scarcely breathe – then suddenly broke away and yelled to the street, 'YES! She's said YES! We're going to get married!' He beamed into the faces of the people nearby. Most smiled. One or two called out a good-natured, 'Congratulations!'

Nobody was looking at the sky any more.

When I stopped crying, I started to laugh.

That was how 'the smiling game' started. The aim was to make as many miserable or serious-looking people as possible break into a smile. On 'competition days' we'd keep count, and the aim was to beat our own record each time – to refine our tactics by experience.

Our methods varied according to the time, place and weather. A woman walking her dog in the rain suddenly found herself the centre of amused attention, not realizing that Driss was following behind her, knees bent, holding his umbrella over the damp, reluctant dog while the rain poured down and soaked Driss himself to the skin. Sometimes he'd call out to perfect strangers as if they were old friends: 'You're looking gorgeous, Simone' or 'Didier says to tell you he loves you' – followed by the enactment of acute embarrassment, pretending he'd suddenly realized his mistake, blaming his glasses, et cetera, et cetera. The antics usually produced the desired upward curl of the lips – at which Driss would murmur, 'Yes – it counts,' and I'd add it to the total.

I can't honestly say I enjoyed it. It made me slightly on edge, that kind of behaviour, in case he chose the wrong person and it was taken badly. Maybe I was just too inhibited. Or maybe he was slightly mad – or had more energy than he knew what to do with.

He used to tease me. 'Be young! You're not forty-seven yet, you know. Anyway, I've taken a vow that I'll stop when I'm twenty-five. I shall suddenly become a very serious, responsible, utterly respectable civil servant or banker or something. How about that?'

'No', I said. 'No – that's not what I want, but …'

'So I have your permission to play seriously till I'm thirty?'

I threw something at him in exasperation – but he caught it, held it to his heart and exclaimed, 'A present! – from my girlfriend!'

I stormed out and slammed the door in the required fashion.

I fumed and cried for two days and stayed away from him. On the third day, one of his friends was hanging around outside the apartment building when I got home. He thrust a note into my hand and disappeared.

'The donkey rides: 4.30 tomorrow.'

By 4.25 next day I was already there, in the Luxembourg Gardens, where the patient donkeys are led up and down the sandy path with tiny children, looking very serious, on their backs.

I saw him in the distance. He saw me see him. Held out his arms. Began to run, beaming. I did the same. Running towards each other like that, as if for a film, a romance – running and running, arms out, towards each other … The sweetest run of my life …

… running, running … till …

… Clamped to a standstill. Clasped in arms like iron. Held hard. Held against a hard body. I struggle, struggle for breath, struggle to be free.

But there are other arms there, holding, fastening. Faces talking in the dark.

'Easy does it. Easy does it, my girl.'

Great hands holding my head, forcing the jaw open. Forcing liquid into the mouth … down the throat … Choking … Trying to pull the head free of the iron hands – great fat fingers between the teeth, forcing the jaw down and still other hands ramming the bottle-neck into my mouth and the liquid burning down the throat and into the stomach, then, as if the body's whole system had changed, running straight out from the stomach along the limbs, melting the muscles to limp uselessness – but warm – warm … Soft now … and the arms not needing to clamp and grasp now, but to hold, support, carry a melted, slumping body.

I've been put on a heap of dead flowers – a mix of crisp and rotting. My rag-doll limbs are attended to in some way. I think they're being undressed. But it doesn't matter. My body's so warm and heavy and the bed of dead flowers is delicious to our nakedness. I'm wrapped only in the word 'sex'. The word is very warm against my skin. Moistly warm.

Even the first time it was good. He was gentle. He loved with his whole body, not just his sex. He loved with his eyes. His lips were soft. And his arms around me as if I were the most precious part of himself.

For him, it wasn't the first time – I could tell that.

Dark eyes are looking down into mine, burning, searching through the indigo light. They are so close I can see my reflection in them. My long face. My neck elongated in its nakedness. Two identical pictures of myself.

'Who are you?' I say.

He continues looking down at me with an intensity that could be contempt or could be the look of an artist devouring a subject for a painting. Whichever, it's the look of a man not at peace with himself. His look intensifies and reduces at a glance. He doesn't even bother to answer me.

But another voice tells me. 'Modigliani. He thought he knew you – you with your long thin face. He was hoping for a little copulation, for a little peace. But you're not her, not the one he wanted … By the way, I'm Gérard – Gérard de Nerval, and, since you're here, I might as well enjoy an act of penetration. Now, lie still and don't fidget so I can get it right.'

I begin to laugh. This is too silly for words. I try to get up. But a squat, white body rolls on to me. I begin to struggle and kick. He's heavy and cross. I want to believe it doesn't matter now, that it's all right to take him to me if that's what he wants – if it'll ease whatever torment he … But the reflex action's too strong: I'm all teeth and nails – until a hand pushes up my jaw, clamps itself across my biting ('It's okay, Gerry, we're here,' says a voice) and my legs are pulled down and held and my arms pinned each side and a foot treads itself across my eyes and I'm blind as I feel the anxious, unlovable body trying to find its way into me.

I want to cry for him.

I try not to think of Lucien.

It's difficult not to. The particular way he's jerking, so the small soft mound is pounded against the bone beneath and all you can think of is the fact that you have a skeleton. And he's small, too small still, for us to feel a thing. And even if I want to encourage him now by giving him the simple human comfort of my arms around him, as I'd done sometimes with Lucien, I can't. His friends have me well and truly Gullivered.

When the pressure from the hand is released a little from my mouth, I whisper to myself, 'Don't worry; it'll soon be over. It's different now. Everything's different.'

I'm weeping, silently. But weeping for him, not myself. Weeping for an unquiet spirit pursuing its restless journey in the dark, trying to find satisfaction for what can never be satisfied. Now. For him it's all over, for ever. All I feel is pity – pity for both of us as he jerks on and on …

It'd been a kind of pity that had made me give in to Lucien, to begin with. It didn't seem to matter much. I didn't care about anything after Driss. Was that how my father had felt? Did Madeleine just happen to come along? – a woman who was lonely and a bit inadequate? Someone to pity? Pity is not the same as love. Pity – the revenge of the heart when its joy has been taken from it.

As he jerks on and on above me and in me, I wonder vaguely if, like Lucien, Nerval had once been a waiter, too. Perhaps it was something to do with having to weave niftily between tables all day that made them jerky. I laugh – and the hand clamps back. Gérard is obviously the kind that has to take it all seriously – has to be *taken* seriously in his efforts.

Lucien had a very small place near the *Gare de l'Est* – one little room with what was really only a single bed, a tiny table, a few shelves, a cooking hob, sink and mini-fridge. A toilet and shower occupied what was little more than a large cupboard.

I moved in with him on a July evening. That first night it was so hot and stuffy, I could hardly breathe. And with the windows open there was too much noise to sleep. Making love was …

joyless. I told myself it was the excitement of the new situation: tomorrow would be fine.

At seven I got out of bed and groped my way around Lucien's shelves for coffee. I worked out how to boil the unfamiliar kettle and made two mugs – a good strong one for me: black. Lucien groaned and turned over. 'What's the time?' 'A bit after seven. Here, I've made you some coffee.' My first 'wifely' act. I was feeling full of affection for the vulnerable-looking human being I'd watched sleeping through the early light.

'Why the fuck are you making coffee at seven o'clock in the morning?'

I felt the blood rush to my face. I wanted to cry. And I was so tired. 'Because it's time to get up,' I said, feebly. He turned over, pulled the cover over his head, mumbling 'No, it fucking isn't,' and the coffee went cold beneath its scab of powdered milk: I couldn't find a spoon.

I showered and dressed with as little noise as possible and left him a note to say I'd gone out to look for a job, as planned. I'd call in at the café later – and sorry I'd woken him too early. And I told him I loved him.

He makes a funny little noise. And it's over.

I wait to be released. But I'm still pinned to the ground.

Then a voice says, 'No. Let her go. There are other ways.'

I open my eyes on to indigo and a naked man sitting down beside me. A neat beard and kind eyes. His body isn't young, but it's substantial. His sex is hidden by his thigh. I can't see whether it's roused. He slips an arm under my shoulders, sits me up, cuddles me to him, rocks me, saying, *'How glorious but how hard it is to be, in this world, an unusual kind of blackbird …'* He's a father telling me a bedtime story – *The White Blackbird* – a story to suit my mood, a story to give me what I need at this particular point. A good and sensitive father. His kindness makes me weep.

But then, from behind, a voice says, 'Get on with it, Grandad.'

'No need to be rude, Modi. Experience counts, you know.'

I'm not sure what he means, but it's nice to feel safe in his arms. He has a soothing, slightly dolorous voice. Putting a hand under my chin, he turns my face towards him and kisses my trodden eyes. Gently he touches a breast, lifts it, bends his head and tickles it playfully with his beard. He looks at me, smiling, as if for permission to go on. What can I do but smile back? He takes the nipple in his lips deliciously. I begin to dissolve in warmth. His hand is between my legs, touching me gently, gently. He doesn't hurry. I feel myself opening to him, lie back on the bed of old flowers and smile his good old body to me. He smiles and comes to me, into me. I'm held in his arms and still he doesn't hurry. Lies still in me, savouring the togetherness of it. Gently he begins to move with a loving motion, smiling into my eyes. He only has to move a little more strongly and I come, come as easily and beautifully as with Driss …

This is how it would have been with Driss if he'd grown old with me … this loveliness of love …

If …

If …

He still moves gently, gently, sometimes a little quicker, sometimes a little slower. He's pleased with his skill, I can tell. Moving … making me feel the love he feels for what he's doing … gently … gently …

The puppet theatre in the Luxembourg Gardens. 'The beginning of moral education for middle-class Parisian children,' as Driss called it. Timeless ingredients – goodies, baddies, fear, violence. Its main fault was that the goodies always won: a foregone conclusion. It's how they won that kept us interested.

We hadn't known each other long. We were walking through the Luxembourg one afternoon when neither of us had classes for some reason – I think it may have been a teachers' strike – when we heard the bell. We both stopped dead in our tracks and said, 'The puppet man!' at exactly the same moment. Then we laughed – partly from the memory of childhood excitement at the sound of that summoning bell along the paths under the trees (it meant the show was about to begin) and partly because we were 'seriously' in love and beginning to realize it.

And we decided we'd probably been in the puppet theatre at the same time at least once in our childhoods – despite the age difference: I'd started going at the 'minimum' age – and he carried on until 'quite old' because of his little cousin. And we started reminiscing as if we were a couple of wrinklies.

'Which one did you like best?' '*The Three Little Pigs*. What about you?' '*The Nightingale and the Emperor of China*.' 'There was always a crocodile or a wolf, wasn't there – and usually both. Or am I just muddling them all up?' 'The baddies always had big white teeth, I know that much. I used to dream about those teeth.' 'I always thought the goodies should've had the big teeth.' 'Nietzsche would've sided with the wolf – you realize that, don't you?' 'Why do we teach kids goodies and baddies when none of it's as simple as that?' 'It's funny, isn't it, the way we start off with it all clear – black and white – then we come to think it's all just a grey mess. But then there comes a point when we can't go along with relativism any more and it's "foot down" time – time to stick up for certain things…' I could have listened to him for ever – looking into the thoughtful brown eyes behind the serious glasses, watching his soft mouth move, his white teeth (two at the bottom slightly crooked).

I knew from that day there was no one else I wanted to spend my life with. We hadn't even slept together then.

Sometimes – afterwards – I used to go and sit near the puppet theatre and listen for the bell being rung and watch the children going in. I'd look out for beautiful little boys with dusky skins and hope they'd …

Voices.

I open my eyes. Hers are still closed. After all the business with the body, I'm splitting from her again.

Voices raised. Some kind of commotion just out of eyeshot. So the guards have found me, have they? I force myself into a sitting position. The girl remains prone, eyes shuttered.

There's a struggle going on. A fight? In the violet gloom, I just make out the swirl of Oscar's cape, Apollinaire's bandage. My eyes adjust … to see Nerval, Musset and Modigliani being frogmarched from the scene.

What, in my confusion, I take to be a guard's face is close to mine – broad, mannish face, strong nose …

And he's wearing a dress.

I leap away, utterly separate again.

Now *she* stirs and begins to open her eyes. I laugh softly at her. She thinks she's waking from the dream and will find herself by the Héloïse and Abelard tomb, the gun in her pocket. She thinks she fell asleep and that the guards have found her. 'So be it,' she's thinking. 'Face the music.'

Two figures in front of me.

'God be praised!' (A tiny, sparrow-like woman.) 'Her eyes are opening!'

I blink into the deep purple dark, smelling the heap of dead flowers with their odour of sex. An aging woman on either side of me.

I try to close my eyes once more. How long before the nightmare ends?

A strong hand shaking me and Stein's American voice says, 'Come on, dormouse, come on. Stay awake – stay *awake*.'

'But I'm not awake.' (Such a thick effort to talk. Tongue big as a cow's.)

'Yes you are. You've just had too much to drink, *chérie*.' A rich French accent, so different from Stein's American voice.

Then Gertrude again. 'Stand back, Edith, stand well back, sparrow. She'll no doubt throw up once she comes round – comes round properly.'

At which point I do, in fact, vomit with impressive violence –
almost with enthusiasm, as if ridding myself of all the ills within
me. Left with the taste of bile. My drained, my utterly emptied
body. An odd tenderness for it.

Driss didn't drink. He said he could be daft enough without
alcohol to help him. Besides, it just gave him a headache and
made him feel terribly, terribly sad. The only time he'd drunk a
lot, he'd cried all night, he said – though I had to promise not to
tell his friends (about the crying, that is). So I didn't drink, either,
except a little wine at family meals.

With Lucien it was different, of course.

I went through a stage of having no will of my own – which
is how I got involved with Lucien in the first place. He just came
along and at the time I simply didn't care enough to shake him
off. One evening he got me drinking – 'seriously' drinking – and,
because I wasn't used to it, I was quickly in a condition where I
didn't care what he did … Banal.

A tedious little story of waking up naked in someone else's
bed, a whiff of unfamiliar sheets, the curve of an unfamiliar spine
turned towards you in a foetal sleep.

And after the first time …

I felt sorry for him. He was nice, really. If he'd had proper
chances in life … he couldn't help it.

But sometimes I wished I hadn't got involved – even to
'punish' my family (which is what they claimed I was doing). I
just felt so sorry for him.

But I didn't love him.

If only I could've just rid myself of the whole thing – vomited
up the entire relationship and started from where I'd left off.
Even without Driss.

If only. If only. Purgatory in two words.

Once I recover from it – the vomiting – I begin to feel better.

'Let's get you away from here, right away.' Gertrude's strong arms help me to my feet. Legs like warm water. The tiny sparrow-woman holds my left arm.

'You all right there, Edith? – you all right? Not too heavy for you?'

'I'm stronger than I look, Gertrude.' A rich, if slightly nasal, voice, exaggerating every 'r'. A voice much bigger than the woman.

'Where are we going?' (A whimper from this limp, naked body of mine.)

'Not far, *chérie*. There are some steps nearby. We'll sit there for a while, shall we?'

'Nicer than sitting next to your own vomit. Anything's better than that, isn't it? – better than vomit … sitting next to it.' (Gertrude.) 'Now, come on. Let's get you clothed in your clothes before you die of cold.'

I feel their hands dressing the rag doll that I feel myself to be. Stein's hands are strong for pulling and pushing. Piaf fiddles with buttons and zips and tucks things in.

It's done at last.

They lower me gently on to stone steps.

'So, my rose, what are we going to do about you – what *are* we going to do?'

'What do you mean?' My voice is flat: I no longer have any real interest in the problem of 'myself'. It's all drained away – the readiness to feel, react, be offended, angry. I'm oddly happy, though tired, so tired.

It's Edith Piaf taking my hand. 'Why are you here, *chérie*?'

'Why am I here?'

In the space before me, the past plays itself over and over in miniature, scenes overlapping, repeating, like singing a 'round'.

'Draw me a sheep.'

Naming me 'Zade'.

Walking. Talking. Reading. Joking.

Falling out. Making up. Making love.

Meeting his family for the first time. (He never met mine.)

His father Moroccan. His mother French.

Telling Driss, 'If I were forty, I'd be in love with your father.' Driss giving me a funny look. Such a lovely man, his father. But tall – taller than Driss, who took after his mother.

And poetry, always poetry. The night he shouted, '*My love is like a red red rose*' (badly pronounced) from the window at two o'clock in the morning – me trying to drag him in, pleading with him to stop … Threatening never to help him with his English again.

Meeting his Sorbonne friends for the first time. Telling me how he wanted to be a teacher and that his mother said he should aim higher. His father said he should do what he wanted.

Middle of the night.

Ringing and banging on the door. Start of the nightmare.

My father … Fighting past him.

His brown hand in my white hand.

His hand in mine.

'Never. Never. Never. Never. Never …'

The words of King Lear over his daughter.

Is that how my father will react when … if … ?

Into the space before me, where the past is dreaming itself over and over, runs a cat. Like a stone cast into a still, dark pool that mirrors the moon's gaping face, the images fragment, tremble into pieces, disappear – mercifully – for a moment. Mottled violet, the cat rubs against me, then climbs on to my lap and curls on to the anorak. I stroke its head, absent-mindedly, gently, as if it's the head of a lover … The cat purrs. In the clear space the past reassembles itself once more, like spilled mercury collecting – a silver film with violet shadows. Fragment of a nightmare. Over and over.

Two o'clock in the morning when his friends came to our apartment. A policeman with them. My father roused from his bed and finding two 'Arabs' at the door – then his darling daughter refusing to go back to her room, throwing on a coat and fighting her way past him (and all the time Madeleine shouting in the background), his 'little girl' running off into the night to be with her lover …

'*Chérie*, you seem to be losing yourself into the past. Come back to us. Tell us why you're here. Is it a problem to do with Love, by any chance?'

Piaf's words scatter the scene. A relief to stop reliving that nightmare. More than a relief: a mercy.

Mercy. Its five letters form softly on the lips of an angel, gently blowing the worst of the past away … for the moment.

'Yes. Love. A problem of love.'

A picture drops into my mind. Of a hand that lays down two playing cards – the first a stylized picture of a beautiful dark young man holding a book; then over it is placed one of a white waiter balancing a tray on his palm. This second card's at an angle and only half covers the first.

'A young man?' prompts Piaf.

'Yes,' we say.

'And he was unfaithful to you? It's an old story, *chérie*, an old story, this love, this being left by a man …'

Is it the love in popular songs she's speaking of? *Chanson* love? (If it were *only* that!)

And it strikes me afresh how these people, these 'presences' – whatever they are – hold the essence of their earthly selves, their afterlife nothing more than a precise, concentrated shadow mimicking their lived lives. Little in the way of compensation or enlightenment. No cleansing or metamorphosis. The occasional flash of greater objectivity, perhaps – fleeting views of one or two details *sub specie aeternitatis* – that's all.

Which made the lived life terrifyingly important.

It's what we're stuck with for eternity.

All there is.

Visceral the great cry of anguish that rises from my stomach, through my lungs, forces itself out through my mouth.

AM I DEAD?

AM I DREAMING?

WHAT DOES THIS MEAN?

Never moving on. Never able to contribute more – or less – to the world. Except through others, and then it might not be what one intended at all. Look at Nietzsche …

… But it's Piaf I'm looking at. She's the words of her songs packed into a small body with strangely large and mannish hands. I see the sex of her reddened lips, the moist emotion of her eyes, the dark brittle halo of hair like a tragic memory always there (that plane crash, the loss of the one she loved …). She's over. Complete. Contained in a frame.

Would he put my photo in a frame – my father – and keep it on his desk at work? – his colleagues touched, embarrassed. Saying to each other, 'So tragic, to lose his daughter like that, on top of losing his first wife. Poor man. He puts on a good face but you can see it's really affected him. As a parent, I suppose one must always feel responsible, even when it's nothing whatever to do with you …'

Or would he and Madeleine simply bag up my stuff – my books, my music, my poetry, my postcards and letters – bag it up and put it out as garbage?

Condolences offered, would my father just shrug and say, 'She got in with a bad lot, I'm afraid. Fortunately, my son …'

No! *NO!*

Oh, Papa, why did you have to … ?

Why couldn't you have … ?

If only I could believe in the myth of my mother waiting for me at the gates of some heaven, even my mother carrying my limp body, my limp soul, like the *Guernica* mother, gazing up to a heartless sky, mouth terrible with anguish …

Stein's looking at me with such motherly compassion that I begin to weep. But the words that come out of me are nothing to do with the mother I never knew.

'I want him. I *want* him. My arms ache with emptiness; every inch of my skin pines for his; my feet for his feet; my fingers for the feel of his knuckles, his nails. I long and long for the feel of him in me. To touch his hair. See his eyes – asleep, waking, awake.'

'And the voice, *chérie*, the voice?' Piaf takes my hand.

'Oh, *yes* – the voice – above *all* his voice …'

(*'Draw me a sheep …'*)

'Come on now, my lamb, this won't do, won't do at all …' Stein hugs me as if willing her strength into me.

(*'Draw me a sheep …'*)

'But I feel so lonely.'

'We understand, *chérie*, we understand …'

Do you? Do you really?

(*'Draw me a sheep …'*)

That summer he was Virginie Durand, he was Claudine Belhomme, he was Justine Lacoste – the three new friends who wrote to me frequently while we were in Normandy. Virginie had a very plain prose style, a small, rather pinched signature, favoured a sober font and cheap brown envelopes. She often wrote about politics. Claudine was a great reader. We corresponded regularly about books. Her signature was fancier than Virginie's and she sent her letters in those nice grey envelopes lined with tissue. Justine was the only one who wrote by hand – wild, energetic writing with lots of exclamation marks. With her it was all other people's romances, wild 'scrapes' and the latest jokes doing the rounds among 'her' friends.

It made those weeks away from him tolerable.

I didn't have to worry about hiding the letters – nor the fact that I was replying. As far as the family was concerned, Virginie, Claudine and Justine were three new friends and 'very good for me' (I heard them say so: 'She looks so happy! She's really blossoming …').

'These new friends of yours, you must invite them round when we get back to Paris,' said Madeleine. 'It's nice that you've got some proper friends at last ... not just that Marie-Odile girl ...' (Madeleine: sensitive as ever.)

So I'd have to engineer 'falling out' with them, probably by mid-September ...

Our Normandy house had belonged to my mother's parents – whom I never knew. Madeleine's resentment that my father still loved the place was overcome by the status of having this very pleasant, spacious country retreat a convenient distance from Paris.

The tree from which Pierre and I used to swing as children (the seat had finally rotted through, one bit dangling from each of the fraying ropes) now became my 'study'. With a couple of strategically placed cushions, you could stay up there for hours. 'Claudine Belhomme' had set me a reading list for the summer ('You're my first pupil!' 'You're absolutely determined to be a teacher then?' 'Absolutely.' 'So I've really got to spend my life with a teacher?' 'Yes, I'm afraid so ...'). So I went up into the tree and I read and read – poetry (Baudelaire, Rimbaud, Verlaine, Prévert ... even some Shelley and T. S. Eliot in English) and novels (*La Peste, Les Enfants Terribles, La Nausée* ...), ploughing through the list, determined to impress him – writing about it all to Virginie/Claudine/Justine at the addresses he'd arranged with friends.

I was terrified he might meet someone during the weeks I was away. Someone less plain, someone who didn't have to adopt all the stratagems of secrecy ...

'Are you going to spend the whole holiday up that tree?' grumbled Madeleine, when I declined to go with them to Bayeux again.

'Really – I'd rather stay here …'

It meant I could walk into the village and use the phone box. Using the house phone was out of the question (it'd show up on the bill) and I didn't have a mobile.

We only managed to talk three times over the Normandy weeks, and each time left me in a turmoil of elation and terror. When I asked him, 'What've you been doing?' he seemed to guess from my voice that what I really meant was, 'You haven't been seeing anyone else, have you?' So he'd tease me. 'Oh, I've put an ad in a lonely hearts column' or 'Last night I slept with Justine Lacoste – quite a girl!' or 'Well, you know – the usual things us young males get up to – sleeping around …'

'Driss – stop it …' He might have heard laughter in my voice, but did he catch its tearful edge?

'And what about you?' he said once. 'Have they paired you off with some nice respectable boy with a big house in the country?'

'Driss – stop it!'

Until then it'd never occurred to me that he might be feeling as insecure as I was about us being apart. He knew he wouldn't be the 'son-in-law of choice' for parents like mine. I suppose he was afraid I'd be too weak to resist their pressure.

Maybe he had more to worry about than I did.

He wasn't puritanical when it came to sex, but he certainly wasn't into sleeping around. He said it was often another form of exploitation. And why take the risks that came with it? What satisfaction could there be in a relationship that didn't involve 'the whole person'? Anyway, it was old-fashioned, all that sixties stuff: just doing it because you could, because of the pill et cetera.

When I said I thought he wasn't a typical young male, he said some men were fed up with that insulting attitude to them.

Okay, none of his friends were virgins, but they wanted whole relationships: sex was sex – give or take a few details – but having friendship, companionship, a sharing of life at all levels: that's what most of them were looking for, in their heart of hearts. 'They envy me,' he said, 'because they see I've found that. At least, I thought I had; but if you don't …'

'Driss – STOP IT – *PLEASE* …' Sobbing, 'I love you – I love you … you don't know how much I love you. It's just … other people put ideas into my head and … I get afraid.'

A pause. His voice very quiet. 'Don't be afraid. Never ever be afraid – of anything.'

Chère Claudine,

I've just finished *La Nausée* and although I found some of it interesting and relevant (like the bits about the root and the hand), I must admit I thought Sartre's attitude to the Autodidact was appalling and marks the book as quite old-fashioned in some ways. I can see what he's trying to say through the character, but even so. Anyway, attached to this letter is a sheet with my responses to particular pages and ideas – as you suggested. I hope you won't find them too naive. You're so much cleverer and more widely read than I am.

What have you been reading/doing? Please write very soon – I'm desperate for letters from you out here in the countryside. Fortunately Virginie and Justine have been writing quite often, too. If you see them, give them BIG kisses from me.

Can't believe how lucky I am to have met three new friends I get along with so well. Thank you for letting me be part of your group.

Sorry about the nasty smudge on this page. A bird has just crapped on it (I'm writing this up a tree).

Hope this has been forwarded to you from Paris. I lost your holiday address.

Je t'embrasse,
Zade

'Your mother used to sit up in that tree when she was a girl.' My father looking at me in a strange way. (Was I growing more like my mother?) 'There's a photo of her …'

If I was very still, the starlings would come and settle in the tree at a certain time in the afternoon, bringing their common chatter and shiny cheerfulness – a counterpoint to my intensity as I devoted the summer days to Baudelaire, Gide, Camus, Yourcenar, Rimbaud, Prévert …

A head full of starlings and poetry.

Starlings and poetry.
S … P…
What was I thinking of?
S … P … – of course.
Stein. Piaf.
(That's silly. Because it's Piaf that's the bird. She sings. Piaf. Sparrow. Little bird.)
Stein. Piaf.
They are women. They are small. They were not afraid.
I am a woman. I am small. I will not be …

Never be afraid. Find a voice. Sing a song.
Let the voice be bigger than the woman.
Where is my voice?
Gone.
What did it sound like?

Forgotten.

Lost shopping list blowing along a gutter.

(Five kilos of grief.

Giant-size packet of memories.

A bottle of longing.

Two large jars of anger.

A crate of if-onlys – 'Purgatory' brand.)

His voice in my head. Singing off-key, and dancing to an old Georges Moustaki song –

Nous avons toute la vie pour nous amuser –
Nous avons toute la mort pour nous reposer –
Nous avons toute la vie pour nous …
Nous avons toute la mort …

… all of life to enjoy ourselves … all of death for resting …

Over and over –

La vie.

La mort.

Life.

Death.

I'm Schrödinger's cat – alive and dead at the same time.

Which do I want to be? Do I want to have eaten the poison the world's provided? I don't know – don't know my own mind any more.

Hello, mind. Are you receiving me?

Hello, brain. Are you still there?

Where's that head full of poetry and starlings?

What's *happened* to it?

A screen. On it projected a complex, chaotic pattern – a multicoloured fruit high-speed splattered against glass. A voice inside me (I think), the kind of voice that would wear a clinical white coat, is pointing to the screen with a long stick and telling me this is my brain. I tell the white coat there's been a mistake: that's not my brain – it's a painting by Jackson Pollock. But the white coat ignores me as if I've said something too silly to warrant a response. So I look again. I look and look but can make neither head nor tail of the pattern. Look and look and still none of it makes sense.

But the hand at the end of one of the white sleeves adjusts a knob on a piece of electrical equipment almost out of eyeshot. The screen is changing. I gaze at it and start to smile. The voice in the white coat stands back, silent – smiling, too. The kaleidoscope has been magically adjusted – a little turn to exactly the right place. What I thought was just a tangle of colours settles into a picture. A crowd of people. The inhabitants of my brain …

Words begin to bubble up from their mouths – more and more, adding phrase to phrase, sentence to sentence, airy accretion of words like clusters of shining bubbles rising from water run fast on to bath-foam – more and more, resting on each other, growing out of each other, a mass of other people's words and thinking turned to an enormous iridescent walnut: my brain.

Part of me despairs to see myself as nothing more than this conglomeration of others' words and visions. And part celebrates the fact that no other human being is made of exactly this cocktail of ideas and influences in exactly these proportions. As the word I-N-D-I-V-I-D-U-A-L-I-T-Y comes up in lights across the top of this picture of my brain, I look hard at it to make sure there's no mistake. Yes, there it is, INDIVIDUALITY – up in razzmatazz bright city lights – flashing on and off, on and off. Beneath the lights, people stream out of a building – a gigantic purple cinema – stream towards me, smiling, waving, nodding as they pass. I know every one of them, this carnival collection – the writers and artists and film-makers and thinkers, along with the people and images they created and which have crept into me through eyes and ears. Streaming past. I recognise them all, though I've forgotten some of their names now, heroes and heroines from childhood books devoured in a single evening … adventurous tomboy girls, and maidens in towers awaiting rescue, a white blackbird … And those with unforgettable names – Babar, Asterix, Tintin and, of course, my Little Prince. Books from an English aunt give me Alice (still in Wonderland), Meg, Jo, Beth and Amy from *Little Women*, and passionate Cathy from *Wuthering Heights*.

But there's no order to the crowd surging past whose conversations reach me in fragments and are scarcely interrupted by their nods and waves and occasional smiles in my direction as they move on: Montaigne is surrounded by characters from Pagnol; Plato follows hot on the heels of Emma Bovary; Anna Karenina chats about love with Colette as they saunter past; Sartre and Abelard are deep in discussion, while Queneau's Zazie pulls Aristotle's beard and swears colourfully at Racine. Camus and de Beauvoir walk side by side in strained silence, though Françoise Sagan is getting on like a house on fire with Shakespeare and Samuel Beckett. Dante and Ivan Denisovitch swap images of their own private hells. Héloïse is giving Voltaire a good talking-to. In the middle of a crowd of characters from Balzac, Molière and Oscar Wilde are telling jokes, and Chekhov's three sisters dab their eyes as a little girl from Zola tells her heart-rending story. Gertrude Stein is rabbiting on to a bemused Pascal, and Rousseau is clearly not impressed by Proust's account of the family walks along one of two possible little local paths. Apollinaire is trying to get Thomas Mann to lighten up a little. And there's Gide, and Victor Hugo, and Stendhal, and Le Grand Meaulnes himself …

There's a great knot of poets, some bickering over theories and manifestos, most with bleeding hearts on their sleeves, a few carrying violet silk banners on which my favourite lines stream, luminous, in a fresh breeze above our heads …

Il pleure dans mon cœur
Comme il pleut sur la ville.

… weeping in my heart as it rains on the town.

My love is like a red red rose …

... A la main une fleur qui brille,
A la bouche un refrain nouveau ...

... a shining flower in her hand, a new song in her mouth ...

Au calme clair de lune triste et beau,
Qui fait rêver les oiseaux dans les arbres ...

...moonlight – calm, sad, beautiful – which makes the birds dream in the trees ...

And weaving through this great crowd are the artists and pictures I'm made from – pictures by Cézanne, Kandinsky, Chagall, Degas, Dali, Gauguin, Munch, Van Gogh, Picasso, Manet, Klee ... their people and creatures and objects carried above our heads – old chair, apples, melon slice, melted clock, rainbows ... rainbows ...

And so many more ... so many more ...

And teachers and friends, and the writers of textbooks whose faces are blank but who carry placards of what they've taught me ...

More and more and more until the pressure building up in my head is unbearable – too much in my head pressing out against my skull ... people and people and people and people ... fuller and fuller until I'm sure it will crack from the crowd, from the pushing ... the pressure ... the pushing ...

A jagged crack in the skull like a zigzag of lightning ...

And with a huge clap of thunder, the pressure's released. The deep purple sky above the cinema crowd explodes into a downpour of rain so sudden that the air is full of screeching and they all scatter for shelter ...

That walk in the Bois when it rained so hard everyone else ran for cover – but me. Hair darkened, flattened with it, rivulets running down the back of the neck. Stinging cheeks. Alone. The cold rain …

Somewhere to the left, voices are calling me in from the storm in my head. I turn, and see one of those tombs like a miniature chapel or an elaborate sentry-box where some people I recognise are huddled together. They beckon and call, draw me towards them.

I can't read their faces in this purple light. Are they wanting to punish or comfort me?

They're pulling me in – into my own mind (is it?). Into that purple picture I go, and follow an adventure among my spirits.

Where had I got to?

Yes. Here. Sitting on cold steps between two women who know about love. So they say. Will they be able to help me?

I've told them my story. The story of Driss. Of our love.

Love.

But what kind? Agape? Eros?

Too simple. It says nothing of living in the same intellectual territory – unless you count the mind as erotic. And unless you count affection for and admiration of the loved one's family as erotic. Not selfless love, after all. Having more to love than the beloved's self.

Driss was called after his grandfather – the one who'd been in prison. He told me about him – proudly – the second time we met. Proudly because it wasn't for doing anything wrong. It was 1961 – the time of the Algerian war. He'd helped organize a protest – what was meant to be a peaceful protest. His grandfather was, above all, 'a man of peace'. It was written on his tomb. Many of his friends were Algerian. Two hundred Algerians were massacred on the streets of Paris.

It's interesting, what you're not told by parents, teachers.

Many of the bodies ended up in the Seine. The tourist boats must have passed over them.

Driss's father was the eldest of three sons. He was a larger, slightly stooping version of Driss. His manner was very calm and reassuring – a man who was sure enough of himself to be reassuring to others. I envied Driss the dignity of his father.

His mother was younger. A small, sweet-faced lady with an infectious laugh. She'd been out of Paris on business when it happened. That's why it was me beside Driss, holding one hand, and his father opposite, head bowed, holding the other.

On the day of the funeral she came up to me, hugged me, thanked me for being there, at the hospital, in her place.

You could see how much his parents loved each other.

I read a story once about a couple who lose a child: the tragedy puts such a strain on their relationship that their marriage is destroyed. But with Driss's parents, it seemed to make them even more tender towards each other – which only increased my grief, because I imagined the future of tenderness I'd been deprived of by those … those thugs … *those turds* … *That* thug. *That* turd.

'So, my angel, what are we going to do about you – what *are* we going to do?'

'What do you mean?' My voice is flat, expressionless. I'm still worn out from the drink, the sex and the vomiting.

'We want to help you, *chérie*, to find your way.' (Edith.)

'My way where?'

'To wherever you wish to be.'

'Wherever?'

'Yes, *chérie*.'

Silent, I stare at the little arena in front of me where memories play themselves over and over in miniature violet holograms that are also big enough to fill my whole mind.

'I want to be in a place where there's no violence, no nastiness. No *betrayal*.'

'Ah – betrayal. The old story with lovers.'

'Not that kind of betrayal. It was my father.'

He seemed to feel for me at the beginning – though he was shocked to find out about the relationship, and there was that big, awful scene when Driss's friends came for me in the middle of the night to go to the hospital.

(A voice, reading: '*"That's not the way one whistles in my family,"* continued my father, beside himself with anger … "Well!" I exclaimed, outraged by my father's injustice. "… I'll leave … I'll run away …"'*)

Afterwards, he told me the truth of how my mother had died.

But that wasn't the betrayal. After all, you couldn't tell a child its mother had had her head blown off by a bomb in a restaurant, could you?

Her violent and unexpected death was the source of his sympathy for me, but also the trigger for a kind of visceral anger I sensed just beneath the fairly reasonable surface of his behaviour at the time.

The betrayal was what I heard him say.

Unsurprisingly, I was having trouble sleeping – even weeks after it happened. One night I'd tiptoed along to the kitchen on bare feet to get a drink of water and the last of the small supply of sleeping pills the doctor had given me to 'help me through'.

They were in bed but still awake – a sliver of light under the door – and talking.

I heard Madeleine first – '… and goodness only knows what it would've led to, Nobi getting involved with people like that. It's for the best, Charles, really it is …' – then my father agreed: 'Yes, I'm sure you're right. It's probably for the best in the long run. If it'd become … permanent, I'd have found it hard, after Corinne.' A moment's silence. It wasn't often he spoke my mother's name to Madeleine. He sighed. 'Yes – maybe it's for the best.'

That's what he said.

'FOR THE BEST.'

Betrayal.

'Your father, *chérie?*'

'Yes – but it doesn't matter now. I don't want to go over and over it.'

'I'm afraid, sweetie, you'll find a lot of that here, going over and over things. The lives of our living them for always there, eternal repetition in a tangled repeating of the eternal thereness of a now that is both now and not now.'

'But even if your father betrayed you, surely your mother …'

'My real mother died when I was one year old. She went abroad for her job. There was a bomb in the restaurant.' My voice is cold, objective, factual, but I feel my face turn to a bitter mask. 'She's been replaced by a stepmother like the ones you find in fairy tales – always jealous of the closeness between my father and me. But she won't have to be jealous any more. She can have him all to herself.'

(The reading voice: '"... *I'll go far away from you to hide my wretchedness ...*"')

'And so you were alone, *chérie*, and came here to die for love, to be with your beloved beyond the grave and ...'

'Edith, I don't think the girl's *that* naive – not naive at all.'

'But her one and only lover dies ...'

'Not dies – is murdered,' I interrupt. 'And he wasn't my one and only lover. After Driss there was Lucien.'

(The reading voice: '"... *One particular night when it was pouring with rain, I was about to drop off to sleep, exhausted by hunger and grief, when I saw a bird land next to me – a bird more drenched, more pale and thin than I would have thought possible ... He seemed to me, at first sight, a really poor and needy bird ...*"')

He was a hard-up waiter from a cheap student café. But 'pure' white. 'SATISFIED?' I threw it in their faces. I told them what I'd heard them say that night soon after it'd happened and how I found them ridiculous, equating Driss and his warm, intelligent family with terrorists. I told my father and Madeleine that, essentially, there was no difference between them and the thugs who had murdered Driss: those people turned their thoughts into actions, that was all.

I told them how poor Lucien was. What a lousy life he'd had. How 'uneducated' he was. But how I was sure they would approve of him because he was WHITE – WHITE – WHITE ...

But who was I punishing more – them or myself?

The disappointment. His stringy white body. The thin penis. It didn't feel like love. It felt like him just jerking off inside me. The only way to go on was to see it as a way of punishing myself for being 'unfaithful' so soon … the flesh still on his lovely limbs beneath the ground …

(Did my father think of that when he first went with Madeleine?)

'Was he a good lover, this Lucien?'

'No. I just felt sorry for him. But it turned out I wasn't the only one offering him "comfort".'

'Sounds like an old, old story, my pet. Men, men, men.'

'How did you find out, *chérie*? Was there a big emotional scene?'

'No. I just came back to Lucien's place after work one day and found her there with him, crying. She was a poor little chit of a girl and she was pregnant. She didn't know about me. I felt sorry for her, really. Anyway, as far as I was concerned, it was all over with Lucien.'

I remember looking at that skinny girl sobbing about abortion – her bad skin and brittle hair – and seeing through her belly to where a tiny creature – no more, yet, than a hunchbacked tadpole – curled in that cave in her body, clinging like a limpet to the dark cave wall. I said, quite calmly (I believe): 'It's all right. I give you Lucien. I was going to leave him anyway.'

In those frightening days after the eleventh of September, I longed for Driss more than I ever had. I needed to talk to him about it – what he thought it meant, now, for the future. Where the world was going. What we should do about it. I needed to believe in the kind of love we'd had, to believe that …

Lucien's response had been a contradictory mixture of 'Fucking Arabs' and 'The Americans had it coming to them' and 'I'm not taking the Métro, just in case.' He never asked whether *I* was. He didn't want to talk about what it all 'meant', what we should do.

The world was suddenly a much more frightening place than I'd ever known it. And I was adrift alone in it. So very, very alone. So terribly frightened. The whole city suddenly seemed so fragile, so vulnerable.

How could that girl there bear to bring a new life into such a world? Though, from the look of her, her own world had been hard and frightening enough. Maybe her body and her ability to produce new life from it was all she had.

'Stay here,' I said to her. 'Have your baby if you want it.' I packed up my few belongings, went round to Aunt Clarice's apartment. She gave me Michel's old room. He'd been in the army for about six months and didn't come home very often. It was just for a while, 'until I sorted myself out' – that was the phrase.

After the initial relief of having made the decision, I fell into a bout of fury – fury to think I'd been duped, treated like an idiot (the idiot I was, perhaps): fury with myself for drifting into such a pointless relationship in the first place.

Like father, like daughter? On kinder days, I pitied Madeleine, too. A demeaning emotion, pity – but it's all I can find for her.

'You sound as though you've had a lot to do with love already in your life.' (Edith.) 'The trick is, to be able to free yourself from the loves of the past and to start again from scratch.'

'How could I ever be free of Driss?'

'Do you know my song on that subject, *chérie*? It might help you to …'

Gertrude mutters, 'Oh, no! Here we go, here we go …' and begins to hum, *Non, je ne regrette rien* … 'Besides,' she adds, 'you pinched that from Stendhal: "Never regret." That was his motto, wasn't it?'

Edith gives Gertrude a withering look: 'So what?! We all borrow from each other. How else do ideas grow? Anyway, that was a good song … and at least it's more interesting than "a rose is a rose is a rose", which is all most people know from *your* …'

'… which at least avoided the cheap sentimentality about love in your *Vie en Rose*.'

'And what would *you* know about love, Gertrude?'

The road is awfully wide
with the snow on either side
(my my what a sky)
with the snow on either side
the road is awfully wide
and she falls back, fainting into the arms of the man from over the sea
(he is the only one who can turn night into day) and the man from
over the sea murmurs dreamily
*   'pretty pretty pretty dear here I am and you are here'*
*   (the road is awfully wide)*
*   and yet it would be better yet if you had more names and not only*
four in one

'Zenobia Amélie Delphine Eugénie? I'll call you Zade, then. Now practise telling other people your new name. Say "Call me Zade." Go on. "Call me Zade."'

I wish I knew why words are wild
  why I am I
  why I can cry
  (my my what a sky)
and the man from over the sea murmurs
  'the road is awfully wide
  pretty pretty pretty dear I am he
  with the snow on either side
  I am here'
Walking along the road made with snow. The moonlight bright. A white dog and the dog looked grey in the moonlight and on the snow. When there was no snow and no moonlight the dog always looked white at night.

The road awfully wide.

When she turned her back on the moon the light suddenly was so bright it looked like another kind of light and if she could have been easily frightened it would have frightened her but you get used to anything but really she never did get used to this thing.

Why do you worry.

I never worry I am kind of foggy in the head and I want to be clear, that's all …

The road is awfully wide …

So I go on weaving the woman beside me out of random phrases half-remembered from her work, stored in a dusty loop of my brain. Random phrases? Not entirely. Making her identity out of my own. *For* my own. (There must be a reason, though, for storing some things and forgetting others.)

Or myself as a pointillist hologram, little dabs and dots of all the thoughts and words that have made me. A three-dimensional Seurat.

And what is this woman beside me like to herself?

How does it feel to love a different beloved? To love differently?

I envy Gertrude's long life, the life she had with Alice – whose presence, she's said, comes and goes, comes and goes. I envy the fact that their skeletons share the same plot of Paris earth.

Gertrude. The comfort of having her beside me. Broad, solid, smiling the smile of one who is serious about what she does but not taking herself too seriously, saying of herself that she was not efficient but she was good-humoured and democratic. (Odd to realize she's so like Driss. Is that why she's here? Here now?) 'If you are like that anybody will do anything for you,' she said. 'The important thing is that you must have deep down as the deepest thing in you a sense of equality.' Which meant liking to talk to all kinds of people and doing it. Driss talking to the schizophrenic girl on his street. Gertrude talking to me now, hopeless as I am. Understanding kinds of love beyond the songs of Piaf and her dismissive 'What would *you* know about love, Gerrrrtrrrrrrrude?'

'What do I know about love?' (One side of her mouth curls into a smile.) 'What I know about love is that the road is awfully wide.'

On the morning of Christmas Eve it began to snow – great soft flakes that soon lay light and deep on top of one another in every place where no one walked or no cars passed. There were bolsters on the window-sills, duvets on the roofs, new white sheets spread in public spaces – the city turned into a gigantic bedding factory, with more and more white stuffing delivered from the huge grey machine of the sky, itself hidden by its own exorbitant production of whiteness.

We'd planned to meet at the Bois – one of the places we were least likely to be seen together. One of our favourite places. Free to put our arms around each other, to kiss, to be as we wanted. We'd both have to be with our families the next day.

I made the excuse that I had some last-minute gifts to buy. Madeleine said she didn't think I should go out in such weather, which meant she expected me to help her with the elaborate preparations for the Christmas Eve meal. Her lawyer brother and his family were joining us and Madeleine was high on anxiety with the need to impress him and his wife – a fairly nice, homely woman, actually, whom Madeleine often criticized behind her back. ('Sister-in-law syndrome', my father called it.)

It was a relief to get out of the apartment with its heavy tapestry of emotions, and into the simple cool linen of the snow. Though twice my normal size with the padding of jumpers under my usually loose duffle coat, along with big woollen scarf, beret, mittens, thick socks and boots, I felt very tiny once I was out in the huge snowy landscape. A stiff little plastic figure in a glass-globe snow-scene being agitated by an unseen hand.

My present to Driss was in my pocket, protected in a sun-yellow plastic bag: *The Unbearable Lightness of Being* gift-wrapped in dark blue paper sprinkled with silver stars. We'd seen the film together but neither of us had read the book. I'd borrow it from him once he'd finished it.

In spite of the thick mittens, my hands were freezing even before I reached the Métro (smell of wet coats, stale piss and that stuff they pump out to cover the smells) and I knew the tip of my nose would be an unattractive red blob. My veins seemed to be running with iced water instead of blood and I just wanted to be in a warm place with Driss's arms around me. Today was 'our'

Christmas and Christmas was supposed to be warm. We were forced into this freezing outdoor Christmas because I wouldn't risk exposing our relationship to the withering scrutiny of my family. It was easier to keep it a secret. Easier to lie.

'Please don't talk about love. It makes me feel so cold. I'm so, so cold. I feel as if I'm turning to dead marble and there's nothing but black snow all around me … snow or moonlight, I'm not sure which. But so dark …'

Knowing it's white but seeing it indigo – spooky negative of a black and white photo. I clasp myself in my own arms, beginning to shiver. The coldness hangs in the air as pictures of cold made from words, made from paint. An exhibition from the museum of coldness in some side street in the labyrinth city of my brain. The words 'Museum of Coldness' form in icicles looped with spiders' webs woolly with hoar-frost. Gleaming against indigo, the words – Museum of Coldness – hang there in utter silence above the exhibits – whose labels are blank: just little rectangles of old snow, discoloured at the edges, small stains here and there as if a minute dog has trotted from one label to another, pissing on each. Recognizing some of the exhibits, not all, I'm absorbed in the looking, as if this will take me away from the cold in my veins and the dead marble feel seeping up my legs like an icy gangrene. There's no special order or logic to the exhibition, though this in itself is a kind of logic, reflecting the effect of cold and the way it seeps and saps and … For the moment I'm entirely defined by it. I enter the museum. The museum enters me.

Dans l'interminable   In the never-ending
Ennui de la plaine   Tedium of the pain

La neige incertaine　　　　The drifting snow
Luit comme du ...　　　　Shines like ...

With the snow on either side

... and a video clip of Dr Zhivago stumbling, small and dark, through a vast and murdering whiteness ...

> a composite picture
> of frozen canals and
> rivers, small skaters
> – Dutch – cold made
> from paint: tangible.
> 'The Old Masters'

'*... the snow's incandescence ... that fabric magically upholstering the Cité ... transforming it into a phantom drawing-room ...*'

> *Lavacourt under Snow*
> Monet was it, that one?
> blue cold stone houses
> – bare, pollarded trees
> (so masterful, that light)
> Yes, Monet. Of course.

'*... cold weather – the high winds, the snow and the rain – the impossibility of doing any useful exploring as long as winter lasted, discouraged further talk between Meaulnes and me about the lost domain ...*'

'During the harsh winter of 1860, the Oise froze, deep snow covered the plains … Christmas Day … snow …'

Pissarro? Or Sisley?
But which is which?
The Louvre under Snow
and other Parisian
coldness, whitenings

'… snow went flying, bursting against cloaks, spattering the walls with stars … snowball comes crashing on his mouth, his jaws are stuffed with snow, his tongue is paralysed …'

Enough. I try to say something. I make a big effort, but my jaws seem stuffed with snow. That light white stuff has compacted itself into a solid, steely weight that stops all words, overwhelms thoughts except the one big thought – the one big question – which, at this moment, is defining itself as two interrogative words, one above my head and made of feathers – 'Lightness?' – one below my feet, made of iron and sinking into the earth as if obeying the pull of gravity at the planet's core: the word 'Weight?'

I don't know if the women beside me see the words or not. I want to explain that this question of the two words has something to do with why I'm here. Something about whether it matters or not.

The snow rammed into my jaws melts just enough for me to say – in a half-gagged voice, as if from a dentist's chair – 'What's the answer?'

Gertrude is attentive, trying to understand. 'But what's the question, sweetheart, what's the question?'

His present to me was Queneau's *The Flight of Icarus*, a romp of a book about a character escaping from the novel in which he's the main character. I read it twice over Christmas. It made me laugh a lot. I had to pretend it'd been a present from Marie-Odile.

The final snow dissolves and runs cold down my gullet, chills the stomach, chills everything the ribs enclose. Only my heart is a little warm still. Just warm enough to go on.

'Does any of it matter?' I hear myself say.

'Any of what?' Piaf looks irritated and bored.

'What we do. What we say. Whether we live or die.'

'Oh please, *chérie*, spare us the "big questions". You have loved. You have been loved. Isn't that enough for you?'

Once I said to Driss, 'I wish you'd make me pregnant.' 'No you don't,' he said. 'Yes I do – because if you ever left me, I'd still have part of you to love.' He laughed. I laughed, too – with my mouth.

Then he turned serious – there was always a kind of 'gravity of purpose', even behind his practical jokes – and said personal life was important, but it wasn't the only thing: it had to be linked to 'an engagement with the wider world'. His father talking in him. Not that he was just a ventriloquist's dummy mouthing other people's ideas. At least, no more than any of us are. He was always thinking. Always questioning things.

Sometimes I wished our relationship was enough for him. The stories you're brought up with, I suppose.

Sometimes I was afraid of letting him down: he seemed to have such high standards – such high expectations – of me as well as of himself. Just once or twice I wondered whether I could keep it up for a lifetime.

But then, when I was with Driss and his friends, talking, arguing sometimes, wanting to do things – their energy and their humour, and their sheer enthusiasm for everything from a good novel to a good coffee, a good law to a good film … I knew it was the only kind of life that was worth anything, the only kind of life I wanted.

'No,' I snap, with sudden vehemence. 'No. Your kind of love *isn't* enough – not on its own. It doesn't solve anything.'

Edith stands up on tiny, indignant legs and adjusts her clothes, grumbling under her breath, 'Solve? Solve? Solve *what*? What is there to *solve*?' And with a dismissive gesture of her little hand, she totters away and is swallowed into indigo.

Gertrude suppresses a smile. 'The voice is fine as a fine voice goes, but voice in a friend isn't all, not all at all. We mind how mindful one is of mind. Mind mindful of words, returning over them, eternal return over words, return …'

But something is happening to my body. It's stretching, contorting, pulling itself apart, making itself into three simple words wrung from the essence of all my sorrow.

'I … want … Driss.'

My whole body seems to hover in the shape of the words for a moment – but a moment long enough to convey the utter anguish of my body's separation from its joy.

Stein reads my body instantly, and it returns to the shape of a young woman sitting on cold steps beside an old friend whose arm is around her shoulders.

'Oh my dear girl, if that is your dearest wish, the dearest of the dear ones, then I will try. If I can, I will. But eternal return brings the return of all. The ungood with the good. If eternal return is … But let's put that aside to the side. His death will be with him, if he comes, stitched to his heel like a shadow. If you have him, you have him having his death.'

'I already have it,' says the girl, 'curled inside me like a tapeworm. It's the colour of restless maggots.'

The three of them were together. They'd come out of a late-night film. It wasn't as if they were in some dark side street or in some dangerous, run-down suburban area. But the weather was foul and there weren't many people about: the grimmest part of February.

There were six of them. They just jumped out of a passageway. Outnumbered two to one, they didn't stand a chance. Kasi told me Driss had made the mistake of trying to talk to them – reason with them. One of them broke his jaw with a massive punch, then while he was down, kicked his head. Kicked it and kicked it. Kasi and Hassan got away with having their faces slashed by broken bottles. Someone must have heard the shouts and called the police. But the gang had run off into the night before they got there. They were taken to hospital, and as soon as they realized how bad Driss was, they phoned Paul and Ali to fetch me.

They weren't caught, despite the detailed descriptions Kasi and Hassan were able to give. The problem is, of course, they all look the same, those skinhead types. Those *Nazis*.

Gertrude struggles to her feet, rubbing her ample backside. 'Moses! Those stones are cold, cold, cold.' Then she's squinting into the darkness. Calling out. 'Hello. Anybody there?'

For a moment I think Stein's going to conjure Driss for me straight away. I know it isn't as easy as that and whisper to myself, 'Not yet, not yet …'

A figure approaching slowly out of the dark. A bandaged head. My heart begins to race.

'No – not yet, not yet …'

He's too tall for Driss.

He stoops to embrace Gertrude.

'Perfect. The perfect man for the job!' she says. 'At least you will be when I've sorted out this bandage that needs sorting out.'

'Had a bit of a scuffle with old Nerval. Humourless creature, isn't he? Passion with *joy*, I say. Terribly sorry, Mademoiselle, but I've completely forgotten your name. Head not quite functioning as it used to. But not too bad, not too bad – all things considered.' He holds out his hand to me.

When I say my name it sounds odd, as if who I am has given my name the slip – someone's loosened the rope that had previously tied me to its familiar shore.

'Of course, of course. Another mongrel among us. English-French. I remember now. I'm Polish-Italian myself. Wilhelm de Kostrowitsky.' He clicks his heels in military fashion and salutes against the slipping bandage.

Who? But I thought he was …

'Don't confuse the poor girl, don't confuse her, Guillaume. Now kneel down so I can see to this bandage that needs seeing to.' (Her hands are broad and competent as she adjusts his dressing.) 'Nobody calls him that, nobody at all. Apollinaire –

116

more marketable, much more. Now, how does that feel as though it's feeling?'

'Much more secure.'

'Good. That's what's needed. To feel more secure. Now, just try and stay out of trouble – just try.'

'You're the mother of us all, Gertie, the mother of us all – not just "the mama of dada".' He laughs charmingly.

I find myself smiling – his laughter's infectious. Looking at him, I feel the essence of joy and energy trickling back through me. The Museum of Coldness has finally closed.

Stein looks hard at Apollinaire, as if she may be having second thoughts. 'You will take good care of her, won't you? Take really good care?'

He salutes. 'I'll guard her with my life.' Gertrude gives him a funny look. '… so to speak.'

Stein moves off awkwardly down the blue steps. At the bottom, she turns and waves – I can just see her down there. I call after her, 'Please find him … please bring him …'. But the short, broad figure has already merged with the night.

Apollinaire offers me his arm. 'Shall we take a little stroll?'

It's impossible not to smile at him. He makes me feel safe. His manly figure. Protective, not threatening. And so very good-looking … in a kindly way … even with his head bandaged. Something between a lover and a father. Solid and there.

A little stroll. That would be nice. A little walking, a little talking. Something ordinary and normal.

One Sunday we went to the Bois – to the part where the lake is. He wanted to do something he hadn't done since he was a kid and his aunt from Marseilles had come to Paris and stayed with them for a week. He wanted to take the little ferry across to the island.

Of course, both the ferry and the island were a lot smaller than he remembered them, and the distance across the lake much shorter. But the sun was shining, even though it was a chilly day.

We walked up the slope from the landing stage and towards the chalet.

'Madame Verdurin entertained there: did you know that?' I said.

'You said that as if she were real, not just someone made up by Proust!'

'Okay, Mr Philosophy – what's real and what's not real?'

'And how do we know life's not just a dream? … Pass. Just enjoy it.'

A wonderful peacock was perching on a wall; its tail hung in an elegant curve, shimmering in the sunlight. At a table on the terrace with its view of the little ferry coming and going between the two landing stages, four people, English – two middle-aged couples – were being brought a tray of tea and a plate of little cakes. The only customers – outside, at least. They were laughing and saying something about the madeleines.

We went to look at the menu, but it was too expensive for us. As we walked back past the English couples, they were dipping madeleines in their tea, even though it was ordinary tea with milk and not a lime-flower tisane.

'So what memory has it unlocked for you?' one of the men said.

'The memory of a perfect afternoon in the Bois with dear friends, and a chilly sun,' said one of the women. 'But that's a memory for the future, of course …'

I translated it for Driss because his English wasn't very good. Then he picked up two stray paper napkins and handed them to me. 'One day we'll be able to come here for tea and madeleines – meanwhile, you'll have to make do with the napkins. At least there's no charge for the peacock.' The kind of silly things you say and do when you imagine a future.

We're strolling along the blue path like the oldest of friends – lovers, even. I look up at Apollinaire and say, 'Your head … is that how you died? I can't remember.'

'No – I survived the war, despite the bad business with the head, but the flu of 1918 finished me off – like so many others. Millions. Little bug too small to see gets into the body and that's it – curtains. And I had so much I wanted to live for. So much still to *do*. Such exciting times in the arts. I *begged* the doctor to save me – as if he had any choice in the matter, poor chap. If only I could have *lived* …'

He looks me straight in the eye. As I look at him, his face has to melt only a little to become the one I love so much. I want to lower my gaze, avoid what I take to be an accusation. (I *could* have chosen.)

But maybe it isn't. Maybe it's simply a gaze so full of longing and love of life … No judgement, no condemnation … He's the essence of what I want my guardian – any guardian (if I need one) – to be … whether father, husband or god …

I rest my head against his arm, to comfort him, to comfort myself. I smile at myself: there's a kind of happiness in my sadness. The strange mechanisms of our hearts. *('La joie venait toujours après la peine … always joy after pain …')*

119

Apollinaire reaches into his pocket and brings out a piece of paper. 'Here. For you. A *Calligramme*.'

I've seen it before – but never felt it in the same way as now. Sad and happy at the same time. Equilibrium. Or equivocation?

'*Des souvenirs* – memories,' it says. '*Mais il y a d'autres chansons* – But there are other songs.'

I look at it thoughtfully, put it in the pocket with the torch.

I feel so secure, wandering along the path with Apollinaire, so content I begin to believe I could accept this as my eternity – if it were offered as such. Despite the accusations of those who had no choice but to die, am I beginning to hope this really is death, not a dream? (How can I tell, though? How can I …) To be taken under the wing of a wise and joyful friend …

And with the thought, a wing appears, arching snugly over me ('*Here the sun does not enter, nor does the wind, nor the rain, nor the dust …*') – a tent of feathers that makes me feel … but I'm losing my stock of words for feelings. I frown a little, willing them back. Ah, there they are, up there, in old-fashioned script, each one written on a separate feather of the over-arching wing … The words 'secure' 'confident' 'protected' 'invulnerable' 'not afraid' 'peaceful'. My eyes linger on 'peaceful'. I whisper the word over a few times. My ears linger on its soothing sound … and inside the sound of the word I hear other sweet noises from memories of living – small breeze hushing in summer-full trees ... soft withdrawing sea of a sandy shoreline ... whisper of pages turning in a silent room ... whisper of white pages turning ...

And the white wing becomes a page curved over, a page being turned by an invisible hand. The page flips over out of sight, baring me to the deep blue night. Nothing between the top of my head and the moon. Nothing at all.

Nothing.

And Apollinaire's gone.

Exposed, alone, I turn in fear – and face a looming figure, a man with a mass of long dark curls (a wig? I'm not sure).

Molière. He looks exactly like his portrait in the book. He curls an elaborate bow – a bow that may hold a hint of sarcasm in its extravagance. As he straightens up, he moves his head from side to side, while a stage-whisper voice in my ear quotes his words: '*Men ought to be different from what they are. But is the prevalence of injustice among them a reason for withdrawing from their society?*' His head goes from side to side, and his long heavy ringlets sway and bounce darkly, sway and bounce in slow motion ... and all his little characters come tumbling out. They hit the blue ground (some on their bottoms with legs in the air, some spread-eagled) then pick themselves up and scamper off into the night like terrified Lilliputians. (There goes Le Misanthrope ... and there goes Tartuffe ...)

I'm still laughing when – thump! – some large object falls out from under his hair. I watch as Molière bends down, retrieves it from the cold path and offers it to me, a malicious black twinkle in his eyes and saying, 'One only dies once – but one is dead so long!'

Sudden dark. I look up to see a black rag of cloud pulled across the moon. I take his gift, blindly.

The cloud passes.

Silver-blue light falls on a dull skull.

I try to let go, but it's stuck to my hands. It isn't a clean skull. Shreds of flesh still cling to it, sticky.

'Whose is it?' I ask, patches of soft revulsion oozing under my fingertips.

'It's Oscar's,' whispers Molière. 'It's the skull of Oscar Wilde.'

Frantic movements, trying to throw it from me – trying and trying – the persistent, sticky flesh sucking on to my own, no matter how I jerk and shake the thing …

… when my eyes catch on to something moving behind the skull's vacant sockets. Tiny bits of brightness. Silvery Christmas glitter.

I raise it to the level of my eyes (though still trying to shake it from me) and look in. With each shake, the glitter whirls afresh – a little snow-scene in a plastic dome, like the one my father brought me back from London that time – I was about seven …

I shake the skull yet again – this time without trying to detach it from my hands – shake it and shake it until the glitter whirls and tumbles in a storm of colliding currents and confusion … then watch it slowly calm and fall, calm and settle, transforming the scene – a stage – to magical silver.

I put my eyes to the skull's sockets and look right in, as if through opera glasses.

Little blurred figures are coming and going in gorgeous colours – sweeping silks … silly bouncing feathers … A small sound of voices. I strain to hear. A new character appears. Says something I can't hear. Sudden burst of laughter from an invisible audience.

If only I could hear the words. I sense it's very clever, very deep, very funny and sad at the same time, wonderful to watch with its colours, movement, surprise moments of such infinite tenderness … that suddenly turn absurd and make the laughter erupt once more from an audience which …

It's Oscar's voice at my shoulder now, whispering, 'It would've been my finest play. My finest. But as you can see, I died with it still in my head … still in my head …'

The colours grow dim. The figures fade. I shake the skull again, frantically trying to bring them back … but the little storm of silver simply glitters, bluish in the moonlight … falling … settling …

Still in his head … still … in his head … still …

Lonely as the earth looks from the moon.

My head's thick with moths. I have mouthfuls of them. They're stuffing my ears. They make a hermitage of my head and I'm the silent anchorite within.

Thick with moths.

They muffle everything.

Is memory a moth and the lived moment a butterfly?

Or is a memory the brighter, more colourful and precise, and the lived moment just a monochrome smudge of confusion?

'Moths are just butterflies that got caught in the rain,' said Granny Robertson. 'Or else they've swallowed some fog …'

Or else moths are the memories and butterflies the stories we make from them.

Or butterflies are the memories and the stories we make from them are dull and colourless compared with what we see in our heads …

It was soon after eight o'clock in the morning when I left the hospital. Stepping out into the roar of a Paris rush hour. A freezing, slightly misty morning with all the colour kicked out of it. Thick white ghosts pumped from the rears of stationary cars and thinner ones from the mouths of people. I breathed in great lungfuls of the foul air: 'Kill me, go on.'

I was so tired. Filthy grey drapes of infinite fatigue closing off the future.

On a black, night-time sea is a little paper boat with a cargo of wishes. The word 'wish' sounds light. But the cargo is much too heavy for the little paper boat. Tiny bright speck on the oil-black bay under a boot-black sky.

Lonely as the small child at a grand piano on a stage and who's made a mistake and has stopped and doesn't know what to do.

Impossible to go back home and face questions and 'scenes'.

I walked and walked, crossing roads carelessly, half-hoping I'd get knocked down. I walked until I reached the Buttes Chaumont and climbed on numb feet up to the little cupola. I'm not sure why. Not sure what I was expecting. I just stood there and looked out without seeing anything.

Solitary girl on a cliff-top, wind pulling back hair and clothes, needling cheeks.

Our future the petals of a dream pressed between the leaves of a book that has never been opened.

Together we were going to 'chase dragonflies without caring what people would say'.

All the dragonflies have gone. Chewed up by rats' teeth.

He died with our future still in his head. I'm left circling round it, a small planet round its untouchable sun, a dull moth round a bright candle, electron round its nucleus.

Only images and never the thing itself.

'Never, never, never, never, never.'

Deux formes ont tout à l'heure passé.

      … Two shapes passed by just now.

Leurs yeux sont morts et leurs lèvres sont molles.

      Their eyes are dead and their lips are loose,

Et l'on entend à peine leurs paroles.

      And one can scarcely understand their words.

      … la nuit seule entendit leurs paroles …

      … only the night heard their words …

… des formes toutes blanches,
Diaphanes, et que le clair de lune fait
Opalines …

   Pure white, diaphanous forms, made opaline by the moon …

   Les yeux sont morts …   dead eyes …

Souvenir, souvenir, que me veux-tu?
         ... what do you want from me, memory?

Nous partons, le cerveau plein de flamme ...
   ... departing, brains full of flame ...

'Brains' full of flame? No: *le cerveau*. Skull. Skull *plein de* ...

... *formes toutes blanches ... yeux sont morts ... le cerveau ... le cerveau ... le cerveau ...*

They've left me on my own with the word 'Golgotha' in my mouth: 'Place of the Skull'.

Weary beyond words, I sit on a black marble tomb, fold my arms on my knees and rest my head on them, praying for oblivion.

My prayer isn't answered. I sense someone sitting down beside me. A little cough, as if to wake me or attract attention. I sit up, elbows on knees, holding my head in my hands, but keeping my eyes closed.

What fresh torture is this? But whatever it is, it can't be worse than Molière's tricks with the skull. What could be worse than being crushed by the utter unrecoverability of what might have been? Dying with the story still in your head.

The presence coughs again. I deliberately don't respond at first – but then suddenly wonder if Stein has managed to bring Driss to me. Numb with the misery of it all, I raise my head from my hands and open my eyes. I can't bring myself to look, though, in case he's unbandaged and I see the terrible injuries kept from me by the swathes of hospital dressings. Or maybe he'll have grave-eaten flesh. Better not to look. But I can't resist reaching out a hand ... just in case.

After a moment it's taken by one colder and clammier than my own. Is it his? It's been so long ...

I raise my eyes slightly and look sideways – but the hand is hidden by the sleeve of my anorak. From the corner of my eye I see a white rose moving, as if nervously twirled in a second invisible hand. A rose? 'A rose is a rose is a ...' 'No!' I cry out inside myself. 'Not Stein again. I want Driss. I want *Driss* ...'

I make myself look up. I'm staring into a pair of gentle but penetrating brown eyes. It's difficult to see properly in the dark with that cloud across the moon, but ... Yes! ... a smallish male figure – a face still forming ... Driss!! – without wounds! I begin to smile ...

But something's wrong. He's got a moustache.

I pull my hand away. It's only Proust.

'You're very welcome, Mademoiselle Zade.' It seems an odd thing for him to say. In response to my puzzled look he indicates the name carved into the shiny black marble. 'We are, you could say, *chez moi*. A cork-lined room no longer necessary.'

I turn away from his sardonic smile. A blue adagio plays in my head, a three-note motif in the main theme making the word 'mem-or-ies' – a stressed note followed by two rising light ones.

As if he has heard the word 'memories', Proust says, 'Light from a dead star'. Is he defining 'memories' or naming the tune? I would call it 'The Still-Born Song of My Life'.

'It's the light – not the star – that's important,' he says. 'The moment itself is scarcely anything at all.'

The terror of this squeezes my mind in its fist. Living. With our backs to the sun, our past is a shadow spread before us: we look and look.

No significance in the star itself, only in the light from it.

The light – not the star …

'In search of lost time …'

… Mem – or – ies … Round and round they go. Round and round.

'Silently we went round and round … Silently we went round and …'

Oscar Wilde arrives out of the blue, pauses in front of us, points at Proust's grave, says, 'How ugly your house is' – and passes on.

Proust makes an apologetic gesture: 'He can't help it. I think he's a little jealous because I'm French. And because my memories are more happy than his, perhaps – though it was a little bit rude, don't you think? – and a little bit hurtful? – even if it is true. We need to consider what we say to each other, don't you think? When something is said it cannot become unsaid and therefore becomes a memory stronger than the moment of our saying it.'

In fact, the shiny black tomb *is* more ugly than one would expect any house of Proust's to be, though I know I'm remembering something I read once about Wilde visiting Proust at home and saying, 'How ugly your house is,' and its perpetuation in memory (from having been recorded in writing and passed on and read over and over until it becomes part of the memories of so many people) makes of it a lasting point of light long, long after the event is over. And when I look up from the black marble tomb, the sky has become a deep-blue net curtain scattered with diamante, trying to cover the real emptiness of dead stars, to camouflage the great blackness where incomprehensible forces play out the births and deaths of galaxies.

'*Twinkle, twinkle ...*'

Grandma Robertson made sure I knew my English nursery rhymes. Sometimes I'd forget a line and bits of French songs popped out of my mouth instead so the two languages wrapped around each other like a twirl of striped candy, making something interesting and new out of two old songs ...

Like two cultures meeting and enriching each other ...

Like people of different races marrying and producing beautiful children ...

'*How I wonder what you are ...*'

– How I wonder what you are ...

And as if he heard it as a question addressed to him rather than the universe, Proust says, 'I am one of those who give people memories that aren't strictly their own. One of those who takes you on the one true voyage, not to strange lands but to the place where you have different eyes and see the universe with the eyes of another person, of a hundred others, and see the hundred universes each of them sees, which each of them is ...'

'I'm too unhappy to care about all that,' I say.

'Then you are in severe danger of having your mental capacities enhanced.'

I flash a sideways glance at him.

'Happiness is beneficial for the body, Mademoiselle Zade, but it is grief that develops the powers of the mind.'

'For God's sake! ... I wish you'd all stop *quoting* yourselves all the time!'

'What else can we do, Mademoiselle? It is finished. *Consumatum est.*'

THE END. The music soars to a corny climax. The Hollywood movie is over. It tells us so on the screen – in case we're in any

131

doubt. Or the old black-and-white French film declares '*FIN*'.
That's all. That's it. No more.

A beautiful day in May when we visited Père Lachaise together.
He said it was a yearly ritual for him – remembering the
Commune. We weren't the only ones: there were lots of flowers
by the Communards' Wall. On the path leading to it, we passed a
grave where there were fresh bouquets. Driss glanced around to
make sure no one was looking, then removed one of the red roses
– and from another grave, a white one. I was embarrassed – a bit
cross. It just wasn't the kind of thing 'one does'. I said so.

'And what about shooting people fighting for real *Liberté*,
Égalité and *Fraternité*? Is that the kind of thing "one does"? Don't
you think they deserve a couple of second-hand flowers from the
dead? – who don't know anything about it anyway.'

'Then nor would the dead Communards, according to your
argument.'

'It's not *for* them.'

'But you just said …'

'Yes, I know what I said. Heat of the moment. It's so the
living will see them and be reminded. When I come here and
see that other people – people I don't know – have put flowers
here, it makes me feel less mad, less alone in what I believe, what
I value. There you are: I'm a pontificating, high-minded windbag
at heart.'

'And that's a terrible mixed metaphor – and I love you even
more because you care about things like that and say things like
that and I want to be with you for ever and ever and ever …'

'Ever and ever is just inside our heads. It stops there. Don't you think people would be nicer to each other and try harder to make the world nicer if they believed this is all we've got?'

'Perhaps they need the threat of hell to make them do that.'

'You mean like it's worked in the past.'

'Oh, Driss, please …'

'Okay, schoolgirl: essay question for you. "Hell is oneself": T. S. Eliot. "Hell is other people": Jean-Paul Sartre. Which of these two propositions seems the more valid to you in the light of current psychological theories?'

'Driss, please …'

'Answer: it doesn't matter which, as long as we don't pretend hell's somewhere else in an imaginary ever and ever. That's just marshmallow for the brain: very sweet, but not in the least helpful or nutritious …'

'But I *want* an ever and ever. I want to be with you – always, ALWAYS …'

'We *can* be together, but not in the medieval way you're thinking of it as. We have to change our ideas of Time and Space and significance.' I thought he was about to launch into one of his great scientific-philosophical 'explications', but, instead, he started quoting a poem – the first verse of the first piece in the little book of English poems I'd given him.

'To see a world in a grain of sand
And 'eaven in a wild flower –
To 'old infinity in the palm of your 'and
And eternity in an hour.'

I laughed because of the way he got the aitches wrong, made them silent when they should be sounded, and sounding it on

133

'hour'. I pretended to be a teacher writing a report (on my hand): 'Driss is an intelligent young man but must work harder at his English pronunciation.'

He responded with, 'Zade is a charming young woman but must work harder at rational thought.'

My turn: 'Driss is a very lovable young man, but he must work harder at his height.' At which point he considered I needed punishing. (His height – or lack of it – was a sore point with him. I was hitting below the belt – a sure sign I felt defeated.) He grabbed me and began to tickle me mercilessly – tickled me till I was laughing, screaming, shouting for him to stop, laughing again … when a soberly dressed old man appeared along the path and told us off for behaving so badly, for laughing in the presence of the dead and of those who might be mourning them, praying for them.

Driss stopped for a moment, but still held me clamped in his arms. 'We were only trying to cheer up the dead, Monsieur. But if you prefer, we will pray.' Still gripping me tightly, he forced us both to our knees and began to declaim the Lord's Prayer –

'*Our Father, who art in heaven …*' But then he went on –

'You stay right where you are – up there, out of the way – and we'll stay down here on earth … which can sometimes be rather beautiful, actually …' Then under his breath, 'when there aren't any miserable old men spoiling it.'

The old man walked on grumbling and muttering.

'Don't blame me!' Driss called after him. 'It wasn't my idea. It was Prévert's – you know, the French poet? But of course you know him: you're French – like me.'

I tried to put my hand over his mouth. I couldn't bear the embarrassment of it all. Tears were hammering at my eyes.

'Don't, Driss, please …'

But he was in one of those moods when some unpredictable Beelzebub got into him – as if his thoughts and feelings were too much for him to cope with and thrashed about inside his head, trying to find a way out, making him do crazy things. He let go of me, ran over to the Communards' Wall, stood spread-eagled against it, yelled, 'LIBERTÉ! ÉGALITÉ! FRATERNITÉ ! …' And, for good measure, added, 'NO PASARÁN!' Then he made a loud 'dat-dat-dat-dat-dat-dat-dat' sound, rifles or a machine-gun, jerking his body about as if strafed with bullets, then collapsed with a melodramatic gyration at the foot of the wall, among the flowers other people had left.

I stood there looking at him, just a few tears creeping down my cheeks. After a little while he suddenly jumped up and took a bow, announcing, 'The show's over. The End. A little light applause and you can go home.'

I didn't oblige. When he saw he'd upset me, really upset me, it seemed to purge him of his devils. He hung his head, walked over to me, put his arm around me as if nothing had happened and we walked off together, me trying to sniff without being heard. 'Let's go calling on some talented friends,' he said. 'They're bound to be in.' And he took me on a tour of the famous dead of Père Lachaise – not all of them: just our 'best friends' – making up silly conversations with them, making me laugh, making me love him.

'Oh, Monsieur Proust, I want him so much. I can't describe how much I want him, how it hurts to miss him with my whole body, my whole mind, with my whole *life*. Have you any idea what it feels like?'

Then I suddenly feel embarrassed. Fancy asking Proust if he understands a fundamental human feeling!

His eyes smile, but he keeps his mouth serious. 'I think I can imagine something of what you feel, Mademoiselle.' The kind way he looks at me makes me love him afresh. I look at him and, in the slowly diluting blue light, see that he looks a little like Driss – his expression, that mix of humour, intense perception, generosity, deep seriousness … He's looking at me with love (*Eyes of a familiar compound ghost…*'). I reach out my arms to him, close them around him, draw him to me …

Nothing.

My arms are empty. I'm sitting alone on the black marble slab. Next to me – placed there by some admirer? – a single, half-dead white rose.

MISSING
Laughter.
Any information
please contact
Z. Robertson-Bec

'Draw me a sheep'

Ne me laissez pas tellement triste:
        Don't leave me so sad: write to me
écrivez-moi vite qu'il est revenu ...
        quickly that he's come back ...

A voice reciting:

| *Les sanglots longs* | The great sobbing |
| *des violons* | of the violins |

de l'automne	of autumn
blessent mon cœur …	wound my heart …

Projected on to the screen of a bruise-blue sky is a mask of tragedy with the gaping black of empty eyes and turned-down mouth. The next slide is a crucifix – heavy cream body threaded vertically with red. And we progress logically to a Pietà, broken body in loving arms. Cordelia in the arms of Lear (*'Never, never, never, never, never'*) becomes the *Guernica* mother … Eyes to the sky … Saint Joan at the stake … having to pretend it was heaven but seeing the row of stage lights on a metal beam, and one a spotlight straight on to me (light streaming from heaven), having to keep my eyes open into the blinding light …

A torch in my eyes. Still sitting on the smooth black tomb, I squint into the dazzle close to my face and make out, just above it, a bandaged head.

The worst thing about physical violence is that it stops you being able to laugh.

'Driss?'

Apollinaire looks down at me. 'Sorry – no.'

'It's all right,' I sigh. 'I didn't really think it could be.'

'*Pauvre petite*. You look completely done in – so to speak. You need something to bring you back to life. You need to smile, enjoy yourself again.'

'How *can* I?'

'Let me be your friend. Let me help to carry you to the other side of sadness.'

'How? What do you mean?'

'*La joie venait toujours après la peine,*' he says, quoting himself. 'There's always joy after pain.' Then, with that disarming

Apollinaire smile, he adds, 'If you can bear to put your arms around an old cad like me, I'll give you a piggyback.'

The childlike part of me steps out from my mind and I watch it climb happily on to his back. I've split again. This time I envy the girl, supported there on his broad back, clasping him round the neck, feeling his arms hooked under her legs. A child again. For that grateful moment he's her father, lover, god. She rests her cheek very gently against his bandage – for fear of hurting his trepanned head – and closes her eyes. If only this path would go on for ever, taking her away from the place of the sticky skull … on for ever …

I close my eyes. I'm there with her now, on that broad, loving back – joined again.

The blue is diluting, lightening to the muted green of a fading bruise which glows a little through the eyelids. We're joined in a moment of utter restfulness and peace.

Slipping away …

        slipping away …

After making love, we'd sometimes play a game. We'd lie side by side with our eyes closed and one of us would say, 'What will we be doing at this moment in five years' time?' – or ten years' time, or fifteen, twenty, twenty-five, thirty … The game probably started with me needing reassurance that we'd still be together in so many years.

Once I said, 'Where will we be … er … fifteen years today?' He thought for a moment. 'We'll be in Greece with the girls – an autumn break …' 'The girls?' 'Yes. Isabelle will be nearly four by then, and Cendrine will have her first birthday while we're away.' I laughed. He went on with the fantasy, though. 'And on the evening of her first birthday, we'll go to the local taverna and the patron will be a great lover of children and organize an instant party for her with music and singing and ...' 'Won't it be past her bedtime?' 'Oh, she'll have had a long nap during the day, because of the heat – but she's a very intelligent child who doesn't need much sleep anyway. And we'll teach her to clap her hands to the music and everyone there will adore her and we'll agree it's a much better party than she would've had at home with the family and there'll even be a special cake for Isabelle so she doesn't get jealous and all the people will make a fuss of her, too, because she's so beautiful and fearless and she'll dance to the music and ...'

I'm roused by a noise ... voices ... voices ... an excited crowd. And instruments tuning up. Awake. Apollinaire's jolting me awake. I blink into the bright green light. He bends a little so I can slip off his back. I'm confused. We're surrounded by crowds and crowds of people, all looking expectantly towards an open area in front of the Communards' Wall. At the base of the wall, cheap bunches of flowers and single red roses are in various stages of wilting and rotting.

I have no idea what's going on.

People are climbing on to monuments, making themselves a bit taller by standing on gravestones, but all looking in one direction, trying to get a good view.

A figure runs out in front of the wall and a great cheer goes up from all around us – Apollinaire is cheering, too. I can't see, so he bends right down and I climb on to his shoulders. He holds my feet securely. I'm afraid to hold on to his head to steady myself because of the bandage, the wound. I simply lean forward a little – and he keeps very still for me so I don't feel unsafe.

The man who's run out in front of the wall is Molière. I panic – for a moment: more business with sticky skulls? …

'… *Mesdames et Messieurs* – and welcome to our annual Allhallows Talent Show! To those who've joined our happy company since the thirty-first of October last, all I can say is, you have a real treat coming to you. Some of the world's most famous entertainers. And, for the rest of us, the chance to haunt memory lane' (groans from the audience) 'with some old favourites. And, to get us off to a good start, singing about that perennial problem – *l'amour* – please put your hands together for Monsieur Georges BIZET!!!!'

An invisible orchestra begins the muted, syncopated introduction of the '*Habanera*' from *Carmen* – and the crowd is suddenly going wild with laughter and applause as a bearded and bespectacled Bizet in the dress of a Spanish gypsy girl – Bizet in drag – minces seductively on to the stage area, into a brilliant green spotlight and, trying for a rich, female mezzo voice, sings –

Love is like a wild, wild bird –
It knows no laws it wanders free as air …

The crowd sways to the familiar tune, a few join in …

He ends with a flick of his fan. Wolf-whistles, applause, 'ENCORE!' …

He whips off his head-dress, tosses it towards the wilted flowers at the base of the wall, turns the gypsy skirt into a bullfighter's cape and breaks into a full-blooded rendering of the macho Toreador's song. Within seconds, the audience is singing along, yelling out that thumping good tune, laa-la-la-laa-ing it if they don't know the words, and vigorously clapping the beat.

To – re – a – dor – laa – laa – la – laa – la – laa-a ...
To – re – a – do – or, To – re – a – dor ...

I went to a football match with Lucien. For him it was a normal thing to do. For me it was terrifying and incomprehensible. A feeling of violence just below the surface. The sort of macho culture that was simply alien to me. An experiment we didn't repeat (like the time I tried taking him to the Musée Picasso). After that, he only went to football matches with his friends.

All the shoving and shouting that went on. It was tribal. And there was a group of men just in front of us with swastikas tattooed on their heads or necks. The types that made you feel physically sick just to look at them with their maggoty white skin and their shifty, looking-for-trouble eyes. All I could think of the whole time was that turd who had killed Driss.

All the yelling and swearing and one side against the other – it just made me sick.

The applause and cheering is even wilder now – the audience pulls flowers from graves and showers Bizet with them. He picks up the least wilted of the roses, blows kisses to the audience, places the rose between his teeth and, looking back lovingly over his shoulder at the ecstatic audience, makes a sweeping exit.

It takes Molière some time to quieten them all down. 'And now, *Mesdames et Messieurs*, for something completely different …'

A grand piano appears. The spotlight gentles to a lighter green. The crowd sobers in response to the dewy eyes and long fingers of Chopin. A nocturne. It sobs quietly. Turns everyone thoughtful. Remembering past night-times with loved ones, maybe … (*'Les mains dans les mains … face à face'* … hand in hand, face to face …)

A friend used to lend us his room sometimes. I'd tell my parents I was at Marie-Odile's house, and Marie-Odile would go along with it: she even came round specially once to thank Madeleine for letting me stay with her, as a guest usually put a lid on her parents' violent arguments: it meant she had the peace to study – and we worked well together … Marie-Odile should be a novelist with her powers of invention!

I knew I'd get found out eventually. But I always thought it would be Madeleine checking up with Marie-Odile's mother – something like that.

It was only a student room, but it was clean and airy. The friend who used to lend it to us was Spanish-Moroccan. He was a Picasso enthusiast. A print of *Guernica* was pinned to the wall opposite the bed. He had lots of books on the Spanish Civil War, too.

The happiest room of my life.

The problem with Lucien's place was that it was so small and stifling in the hot weather, but freezing and damp when it turned cold. He'd sleep in for hours at the weekend and I just had to lie there, bored out of my mind: if I got up, it would disturb him. I realized he was tired. If he'd been more robust, it wouldn't have been a problem. He couldn't help it. I felt really sorry for him.

But sometimes, lying there, I'd find myself thinking of that other room, no matter how hard I tried not to. Those other nights …

The nocturne comes to a gentle close. The applause is full and appreciative. It draws us all back from night-thoughts, our memories, back to where we are now.

Without introduction, the familiar figure of Oscar Wilde swirls flamboyantly into the sparkling green brightness. A few chuckles from the audience before he's even opened his mouth.

(I find myself remembering the skull and the play forever locked inside it.)

'As I was on my way to the cemetery this evening …' (a little knowing laughter from the audience) '… I met a man …' (Someone calls out, 'I bet you did!' … Laughter.)

'No – seriously, ladies and gentlemen – what can I say after such music? I don't know about you, but Chopin always makes me feel as if I'd been weeping over sins that I'd never committed.' ('And which sins would those be?' from the front row. Laughter from those who heard.) 'Use your imagination, sir. I do. And I'm always astonishing myself. It's the only thing that makes life worth living.' (A few groans.) 'As I was saying – on my way to the Communards' Wall this evening, I met a very sad young lady …'

I freeze. It's *me* he's talking about.

'A young lady who was trying to live. As we all know, to live is the rarest thing in the world. Most people exist, that is all.

But this young lady had a problem – and it was all tied up with "love". I wanted to give her some advice – tell her that there's so much *else* to do in the world but love …' (The audience is shifting; they're not used to Oscar in 'serious' mode. But, a consummate man of the theatre, he senses this …) '… though I do admit the vast merits of loving one*self*: to love oneself is the beginning of a life-long romance.' (Laughter.) He turns his back, flings his cape to the base of the wall, then clasps his own body so that his hands appear to be those of another person embracing him. An old trick, but the audience loves it. Wolf-whistles. More laughter. But some of the audience are bored, muttering.

He turns to face us again. 'Alas, one's real life is so often the life that one does not lead. However – where was I? – oh, yes, the young lady. Problems with her parents, too, I gather. Her father is English: I imagine him with one of those characteristic British faces that, once seen, are never remembered.' (Some laughter, a few restless mutters – 'Get on with it' … 'You old windbag' … 'Time's up' …) He suddenly looks terribly hurt, terribly vulnerable, despite his size and his fame. He looks wistfully towards me, towering above the crowd on Apollinaire's shoulders. How I want to comfort him – for all the wrongs done to him, for his sadness, his courage, his mean death in a shabby little hotel, for that play locked in his head …

Maybe what I really wanted was simply to comfort Lucien for all the 'wrong' done to him. He was kind and decent, but the way things were, he never stood a chance …

Did I love him? – or was it just a particular strain of 'bourgeois guilt' I was suffering from?

Or will things only change, become more just, more tolerable, if different kinds of people forge deep personal attachments?

Or will that simply make for a lot of unhappy people?

Was I being unkind to Lucien? – expecting him to be something he didn't want to be, or couldn't be? My only defence is that I meant well. Let my epitaph be, 'At least she tried.' Or maybe just, 'Sorry'.

Things aren't going well for Oscar. Molière, sensing the mood of the audience, comes on to the stage and gently guides him out of the spotlight and into the wings – then runs back on, dark ringlets bouncing: 'A big hand, ladies and gentlemen, for good old Oscar.' The audience does, indeed, give him a good clap – more for past glories than for his performance tonight. The applause is partly relief that his turn is over. I share their relief, but for a different reason. I don't want to be reminded. I want to be entertained in order to forget … forget … forget … *('the rending pain of re-enactment …')*

Sudden screaming all around me as a huge noise explodes on to the stage with a burst of smoke. The mist disperses to reveal a young man torturing his body into the violent energy of a rock-song beat. Jim Morrison. It's *Break on Through to the Other Side*. The compulsive beat gets the younger ones dancing in the small spaces between the tombs. From high on Apollinaire's shoulders, I look around and recognize Bellini, Rossini and Cherubini with their hands over their ears and pained expressions on their faces. Myself, I feel gratefully blank. While the music's so loud, feelings are drowned out. Emotion obliterated. Just a throbbing pulse through the body – *BRAUM – BRAUM – BRAUM – BRAUM …*

You know the day destroys the night –
Night divides the day –
Try to run, try to hide –
Break on through to the other side –
Break on through to the other side –
Break on through to the other side –

Without waiting for the screams and applause (and the jeers) to subside, he goes straight into *The End* ... The music's quieter.

This is the end, beautiful friend.
This is the end, my only friend, the end
Of our elaborate plans, the end
Of everything that stands, the end –
No safety or surprise ...

Tears are streaming down my face. (Dying with the story still in your head ...) I feel so silly! Fancy some out-of-date pop lyric moving me to ... I try to wipe my face on my sleeve, but the feel of the coat – *his* coat – against my cheek makes me ...

... I'll never look into your eyes again ...

I'm sobbing so much, I can scarcely hear his last number – *Ghost Song*. Just as well.

When I realized I couldn't even go 'home' any more, that's when I started wondering about whether I really wanted to carry on with my life. Sometimes I used to get depressed thinking about how huge the universe is and how insignificant we are, and I could imagine people getting so weighed down with something like that they'd simply choose to die. There might've been a bit of that in my mind but, mainly, it was about not being able to go back to my childhood bedroom, not being able to creep back under the familiar covers, nor to rely on the open, forgiving arms of an unconditionally loving father who'd kept my place for me in his home …

Not that it would've worked for long – going home.

I had no plan. I just took the Métro out to the Bois because it was one of the places I'd had lots of happy times with Driss and because it was away from the city's noise and manic pace, and away from the sight of other people in love.

I'd taken to wearing my walking boots all the time – my other shoes had worn out and I had no money to buy more. I had another coat, packed away at my aunt's, but I preferred to wear the old anorak Driss lent me the afternoon of that Sunday when … that he lent me the day before he died.

I'd been round to his place. It'd been quite a nice day when I'd left our apartment, so I'd just worn a jumper and scarf instead of a coat. But by the time I left Driss's place, it was raining.

'Here. Put this on. It's not very glamorous, but at least it'll keep you dry.'

'Won't you need it?'

'You can give it back when I see you on Tuesday.'

I took it off when I reached the entrance to our apartment block, rolled it up tightly and stuffed it in my bag in case someone at home noticed and asked about it.

Anyone looking at me as I walked on my own in the Bois that day – the cold rain pouring over me – would probably have thought I was some poor neglected waif, or a drug addict, or a schizophrenic or something – head down, wrapped in my own world, my own grief, my own confusions.

> *A travers les branches du temps*   Through the branches of time
> *J'ai regardé passer ton ombre …*   I watched your shade pass …

My life with Lucien was shrinking away to virtually nothing, but everything about my time with Driss was there, in front of my eyes, on a floodlit stage. A comfort – and a torture.

> *A travers les branches du temps*
> *J'ai regardé passer ton ombre …*

Over and over. Over and over. And each time making the longing greater – to hold him again, to hear his voice, look into his kind brown eyes. (*'Never and always …'*)

When it suddenly started to rain, I put the hood up and kept walking, head down. It rained harder and harder. The ground was squelchy in no time. The few people around began to run for cover. I didn't see the point. To be alone in the cold and the wet. A kind of cleansing. Wash the past away. I pushed the hood back and let the rain pour down over my head. I tramped on, cold rivulets trickling down my neck, making thin chilly fingers that reached under my clothes, soaked hair clinging to my head like a cold dream … half-blinded by the rain on my glasses … trying to turn myself to stone, to rock, to anything that was hard and sense-less, without memories.

'Draw me a sheep.'

'You can give it back when I see you on Tuesday.'

For ever and ever and ever …

Crying in the rain.

Ghost Song fades and I dry my eyes with a handkerchief passed up to me by Apollinaire. By the time I pass it back, Jim Morrison's gone and a new surge of excitement is sweeping the audience.

Someone's spotted 'her' in the wings. The light's changing – yellowing, brightening. Everyone stands up, tries to get the best view. No need to announce her – Molière leads the tiny woman, by the hand, to the centre of the stage.

Piaf!!! The crowd goes wild …

Little Edith and Molière exchange a conspiratorial smile. A musical introduction quiets the crowd; she nods him his cue … and they break into the duet: *A Quoi Ça Sert l'Amour?* … Smiles all around, many jigging a little to the catchy rhythm …

Then Molière exits and it's into another mood entirely with *La Vie en Rose* … Half the audience seem to be humming along to the gentle tune; some murmur the words. I look around. Everyone smiling. A few yards to the left I spot a golden Héloïse and Abelard. He's behind her, his arms around her, protective, affectionate; she's leaning gently into him. In a rosy-gold glow, they're swaying to the music. '… *Quand il me prend dans ses bras* … When he takes me in his arms …' Both perfectly – if briefly – happy.

The crowd's cheering before the last chord has even sounded.

The applause is overwhelming – especially when Oscar Wilde and Sarah Bernhardt suddenly appear on stage with a vast 'floral tribute' of yellow roses (lifted from the fresh grave of a recently dead financier, if we've read the signs right) and present it to Piaf.

Now little Edith struggles to pick up the enormous wreath. What's going on?

Under the weight of the flowers intended for Monsieur Lebrun (*Légion d'honneur*), she staggers towards the inscription on the Communards' Wall, the backdrop to this improvised stage. The simple words carved into stone, 'AUX MORTS DE LA COMMUNE 21–28 MAI 1871'. Her gesture of solidarity is greeted with a roar of approval. And it seems as if the shouts and applause will go on for ever … And a kind of chanting starts up, growing gradually in volume as more and more join in, and the clapping becomes rhythmic to fit it: it sounds as if they're chanting, 'Mak-ers – Mak-ers …'

'I don't understand.'

'You will – in a little while.' Apollinaire's tone is dark: I don't want to know what he means.

Piaf begins to walk off the stage. The chanting stops. Consternation! Disbelief! Calling her back …

It was her little joke.

Of course there's one more song.

She moves to the centre of the stage again and the first famous chords of the cemetery's anthem are heard. Everyone joins in, singing at the tops of their voices in the sunny yellow brightness, singing as if there's no tomorrow …

Non, rien de rien
Non, je ne regrette rien
Ni le bien qu'on m'a fait, ni le mal …

(I'm choked with tears, but I move my lips; quietly, hoarsely, I make myself join in. Apollinaire is swaying slightly to the music, like everyone else. I have to adapt my swaying to his, to keep my balance. My voice is a little stronger by the start of the next verse.)

Avec mes souvenirs
J'ai allumé le feu …

(Apollinaire is swaying so alarmingly now that I have to hang on to his ears – which makes him realize my predicament and, letting go of my feet one at a time, he reaches up his hands to hold mine – his lovely, comforting hands.)

Non, rien de rien
Non, je ne regrette rien
Ni le bien qu'on m'a fait, ni le mal …

My eyes are still brimming in the golden light, but I'm beginning to smile and my voice is loud and clear, joining the others in the great crescendo of the last line …

Aujourd'hui ça commence avec …

But the very last chord is drowned by what sounds like an enormous clap of thunder and a flash that turns everything orange.

Screams. Panic. People in all manner of odd costumes dashing about. Utter chaos. And it's suddenly windy again.

I'm swung down from Apollinaire's shoulders. He grabs my hand and we hurry away down a path, wind pulling at hair and clothes: 'Just don't ask any questions: I'll explain in a moment,' he shouts above the din and the howling wind. 'It's war.'

Panic. Uncertainty.

Figures flickering in the orange light, running back and forth …

I'm pulled through flames.

Even as I run and stumble, half-blinded by seering, smokeless fire, I see numbers dancing around each other in the leaping orange tongues. Two numbers. Everwhere I look. Nine and eleven. Eleven and nine – everywhere …

– 9 – 11 – 9 – 11 – 9 – 11 – 9 – 11 – 9 – 11 – 9 –

A boot in the face.
A plane in a tower.
A bullet in a brain.

That boot in *his* face.
Those planes in *those* towers.
The bullet in *my* brain?
Is it?
Nothing to be done?
All end in flames, then?

Life at home became continuous psychological warfare. In the end, I just couldn't stand the atmosphere in the apartment any more. I didn't want to talk to them – and there was certainly nothing they could say to me of any relevance. They were *glad* it had happened. Whatever they did or said to try and 'get through to me' was coloured, in my mind, by that overheard conversation. And as for my 'brother', Pierre … I suppose he'd finally got what he wanted: me a total outsider – no longer 'Daddy's girl'. I imagined him smirking, even in his sleep.

Impossible to move out until after my *baccalauréat*. Once I plucked up courage and went round to Driss's parents to see whether there was any chance of me staying there – just temporarily. They understood, but were afraid my parents would accuse them of 'taking their daughter away from them'. (I don't think they had any idea what things were like at home, even though I tried to explain. A comparable situation would just never have arisen in their own family.) Besides, they were still trying to come to terms with losing Driss themselves. The last thing they needed was a deeply upset, disaffected girl in the house – I could see that.

I'd go home to sleep, but that was about all. I started going to the café to study after school – the one I used to go to a lot with Driss and his friends. I imagined they would … But I think they found me embarrassing, or they just didn't know what to say to me. Perhaps I was too much of a reminder to them. Anyway, they gradually stopped coming to the café. They found another place, I suppose. Because I'd been spending so much time with Driss and his crowd, I'd drifted away from the few people I'd been friendly with at the *lycée*. Apart from Marie-Odile.

She often joined me at the café. We studied well together. It was a bit like before I met Driss – except that it wasn't like it at all, of course, though she was still trying to keep away from her parents: with her sensitive nature she just couldn't stand their continual arguments, especially being under pressure herself with the exams hurtling towards us. Neither of us had much money for food, but we both agreed that anything was better than sitting through endless, tense meals round the family table.

Lucien started working there soon after we did. It wasn't long before he was slipping us extra coffees and the modest food we ordered came in portions significantly larger than the other customers got.

So it began as a sort of conspiracy – the hard-up helping the hard-up.

Even so, Marie-Odile and I were soon both as thin as Lucien. It was the first time in our lives either of us had gone hungry – and at first it didn't do us any harm. We'd both had eighteen years of good feeding behind us. But after a few weeks, it began to affect our concentration. All we could think of was food. I started taking stuff from the kitchen at night, to get us both through the next day. But Madeleine soon realized what was happening and left an abrupt note on the fridge: 'Either have the decency to eat with us or stop stealing.'

So it was all-out war.

Apollinaire drags me from the worst of the fire, pulls me behind a kind of large, rocky black stalagmite with his name carved on it. Panic! Is he going to disappear into his own tomb? Will he drag me with him? Or will I be abandoned here, in this fiery turmoil?

No. He explains.

'Same every year. At some point that miserable bunch object to the noise, object to being woken from their eternal rest. If you ask me, they just don't want reminding what they did in life. They want death to be the waters of the Lethe – total forgetfulness.'

'Who are they?' I watch the continuing chaos of figures darting about in the orange light, orders being yelled, shouts, threats.

'Mainly old-style military – and people with the same mentality. Going to be one hell of a battle. 'The Breakers', we call them, or sometimes 'The Grimbos' – as opposed to us, 'The Makers', 'The Laughers', 'The Defiant Ones'. *They* like to control, stifle change and experiment, hate anything or anyone different from themselves, resort to violence to get their own way, keep their own privileges – you know the kind. Led by little Adolphe, of course.'

'Adolf *Hitler*?'

'No, of course not. Adolphe *Thiers*. Not quite so bad – but you could say two of a kind. Must be something about the name Adolphe …'

'Oh. Yes. Thiers. We did him in History.'

'Nasty piece of work. Remember the Commune? He ... Talk of the very devil! ...' Apollinaire points out from behind his own monument to where a small, white-haired figure like a pompous gnome in spectacles, with an expression of ruthless vigour, is leading serried ranks of fat men in costumes of many different periods, but all with a similar, self-righteous jowliness about them or a lean, convinced intensity. They carry a motley collection of objects as weapons – long 'sticks' in the form of crosses and croziers, holy books, counting machines, bits of machinery, chains of office to be used as slings and bits of broken stone from anybody's tomb for missiles. A pathetic rabble – but terrifying, too. They look capable of anything, given the chance.

The utter contingency of Driss's death – and its terrible irony. If they hadn't gone to that film after all ... If they hadn't walked home that way ... If a police car had come along ... If the mothers of those thugs had conceived girls not boys ... or had had abortions ... Or if one of them had simply caught a bad cold and stayed at home that night ... (a bug too small to see could have saved Driss).

And that Driss, of all people, should die in a cowardly night-time attack on the streets – not even in some big, meaningful confrontation ... Though I suppose the 'meaning' was simply that we live in a world where people still feel threatened by 'difference' – what they *see* as difference, anyway. It's so primitive – it's like packs of animals. Worse, because we're supposed to be able to think and imagine.

They're there for us – all those books and paintings and films and photographs and music that help liberate us from our own tiny minds, our own little lives – that free us to play in the skins of others. And most people just can't be bothered. They just can't be 'arsed', as they put it.

But where do you start with people like that? – the sort who did that to Driss? It's no good talking to them about 'cultural diversity', how civilizations have always thrived where trade-routes crossed and different cultures met and enriched each other. Yes, I'm quoting Driss, of course, who was probably quoting his father … And if my father had said things like that, I'd have quoted him, too.

What, in the end, was the difference between my family and those killers? Money, security, luck. My family had less excuse. Those thugs were simply the instruments of my family's unvoiced, unadmitted wishes – though they'd deny it till they were blue in the face.

But the fact was, they hadn't lifted a finger to change things.

They were 'glad' it had happened. Even my father admitted it, when pushed. *I heard him.*

And if he didn't agree with Madeleine, he should've had the guts to say so – to stand up for what he really believed. It's all right compromising and being diplomatic over small, unimportant things, but when it comes to something like that, he should have …

But he didn't.

He chose to betray me. He chose to betray the standards of human decency I'd always credited him with. He didn't stand up to her.

I hope that's his purgatory – if not his hell.

Through the wavering tongues of orange light, we watch the ghastly procession of the enemy, the numbers swelling from moment to moment.

My pulse is racing as I turn to Apollinaire. 'If there's going to be a battle, what are you going to fight with? And who's going to win? Is it the same every time?'

'That depends.' He's suddenly serious again. I don't know what he means. He doesn't say what it depends *on*. Then he taps my shoulder and points behind a nearby monument, where a small group is huddled as if to launch an ambush. I recognize Modigliani – who's holding a sculptor's mallet and chisel and looking quite capable of violence. Gradually I realize who the others are, too – all with paintbrushes and palettes: there's saintly, gentle Corot, secretive Seurat, and Delacroix next to Géricault.

'And if you're thinking paintbrushes won't be any good against the stuff *they're* carrying, then you're not half the girl I thought you were.' Apollinaire smiles down at me and tears spring to my eyes: there's something in his smile that reminds me of … Or is it just the bandage, after all?

His lovely, lovely head. His soft lips swollen to bursting. His left cheek pulped by that unthinkable boot that smashed at his skull, smashed and smashed at it so he died with his goodness and his future still in his bandaged head.

Behind the fat men march companies of real soldiers who carry recognizable weapons – and behind them a ghastly collection of mean-looking women whose main implements of aggression seem to be their awful voices, urging on the men in front of them, and fussing with their skirts and hair-dos that the wind keeps grabbing at and disarranging, like the scraggy heads of half-dead chrysanthemums – golden, bronze, white …

I look behind me – and see the tiny face of Piaf peering out from behind a chapel-shaped tomb. She gives a little wave and a smile of recognition. Then straight ahead through the orange light, beyond the 'military parade', other familiar figures are gathering in huddles. The composers are sticking together – Chopin, Bizet, Bellini, Cherubini, Rossini, Charpentier … And a little further over, skulking around in the dark orange shadows, dead leaves lifting and swirling around their ankles, are a nervy-looking bunch of writers – La Fontaine, Molière, Balzac, Victor Hugo, Colette and our old friends Proust, Nerval, Musset …

As the women are passing (with their syrup-and-cheese-grater voices and their powdered and pampered bodies), Apollinaire grabs my hand and, keeping low, begins to pull me after him, ducking from tomb to tomb. 'Come on – we want to be where the action is.'

Do we?

We catch up with the front of the parade just in time to see two figures step out on to the path in front of Thiers, who is forced to stop and raises his hand to halt the huge following that's built up behind him.

A beautiful woman in an exquisite costume of apricot satin hung with pearls. It's Sarah Bernhardt. Thiers is obliged to acknowledge her with a slight bow.

'Delaying tactics,' whispers Apollinaire. 'Give the others time to get in position for the ambush. Plucky little woman.' He smiles appreciatively. (I feel a little jealous. I'd like him to smile at me like that. I'll try to be 'plucky' enough to earn it.)

Beside Bernhardt a wraith-like figure appears, scarcely more than smoke, yet somehow solid for all that. He's even more gnome-like than Thiers – bush of frizzy hair, pointy beard and nose, laughing eyes. Apollinaire anticipates our question: 'Perec – writer. Cremated, poor chap.'

Perec puts on a theatrical, echoey voice (a few stifled titters behind us): 'I am the Sphinx of Père Lachaise. You must answer my riddle before you can proceed.' (Thiers is clearly exasperated, fuming – but a look from Bernhardt encourages him to control himself. What presence that woman has!) 'You must answer my riddle to prove your intelligence, your right to lead this powerful band. I am going to read you a short passage and you must tell me what's missing. It's very easy, I assure you.'

Perec produces a book and reads: '*Crimson, florid, Ottaviani starts inflating … his slowly magnifying body brings to mind a purplish balloon …* Got it yet?'

Thiers himself begins to turn as crimson as the Ottaviani being described. Fury? Or just plain embarrassment that this clown has him beaten? – and in front of a lady, too.

Perec continues: '*And, in a twinkling, just as such a balloon will combust … Ottaviani burst, his body ripping apart …*' (Thiers looking *very* uncomfortable) '*… making a din as loud as an aircraft … outstripping sound.* Still not got it? Tut-tut-tut, Monsieur Thiers. Okay, a little more … *Poor Ottaviani is nothing but a puny, chalky mass as small as a tiny turd of ash …* And if you haven't got it by now, you don't deserve to …'

'Give us a clue,' whispers Thiers, reaching for his wallet (a bribe?), trying to remain dignified while pleading, feeling the eyes of Bernhardt on him, his 'maleness' at stake, and his status in the eyes of his followers.

'Okay. Just one. This'll make it really easy. There'll be no excuses after this.' Perec's mouth twists in a wicked smile. 'Are you ready?' Thiers nods. 'Em see squared.'

Thiers is turning redder and redder in the orange light.

'Time's up,' says Perec. 'The answer's ...'

... it shrieks through the air on the wind as The Makers all yell it together ...

'EEEEEEEEEEEEEEEEEEEEEEEEEEEEEEEEEEEEEEEEEEEEEEEEE EEEEEEEEEE'

It's the signal. Suddenly a blast rends the very air around us – a noise so unimaginably loud with energy that the enemy's parade scatters, everyone scrambling away pell-mell with their hands over their ears ...

All hell breaks loose.

I used to wonder what he tried saying to them – before they knocked him down. When I saw Kasi and Hassan afterwards, I plucked up courage and asked them. But they just laughed at me in an odd, bitter sort of way. Then Kasi must've felt a bit bad about it and said, 'When you're pinned against a wall and being punched by a couple of thugs, your ears aren't exactly tuned in to someone else's attempts at rational argument.'

A failure of my imagination.

What needs to be said to people like that? How do you begin to undo all the stuff that's made them like that?

'It only needs a good man to do nothing for evil to triumph in the world' – or something like that. I remember someone saying that at the funeral – one of his uncles, I think it was. It was a quotation, but I can't recall who from. It should be up in lights, everywhere. They should rip down all the adverts and put that up. It should be carved on every tomb. Do away with all that stuff about being a dear father or a sorely missed husband or a devoted wife and mother.

Des souvenirs. Mais il y a d'autres chansons …
Memories – but there are other songs.

Make it a law that it's carved on every tomb: *'It only needs a good man to do nothing for evil to triumph in the world'* and follow it with, 'Here lies a good man who …' with the option, acccording to what was appropriate: either 'tried to do something' or 'did nothing'.

Split once more, I'm watching myself.

I see a girl crouching behind a tomb, trembling and sobbing so much I can't reach her. Head down, hands over her ears – she's like a child who thinks closing your eyes makes you invisible. (If you're invisible, it wasn't your fault. Not guilty. If you're invisible, you don't have to *do* anything.)

The violence all around her, the shrieking and chaos … She's convinced she's in hell and this is her eternity.

Apollinaire is shaking her now. 'Come *on* … come ON. You've got to join in. You're either with us or against us. There are no fences to sit on here, and no room for cowards. Stand up. LAUGH. It'll give you energy and courage. Come ON, young lady: on your feet and FIGHT!' He forcibly pulls her up. I try to whisper encouragement. 'You can do it … you CAN …'

… at which moment we catch sight of Oscar trying to beat off an attack by three men in the uniforms of their professions – a policeman, a judge, a priest. He's defending himself as best he can. He's warding off blows and yelling at them, but he's clearly being hurt.

'Come ON,' I urge. 'It's *Oscar*. He needs our help. Imagine it's *him* … Imagine it's DRISS and you had a chance to …'

164

It works. She looks like someone suddenly wide awake after a long sleep.

She starts to run, pulling the torch from her pocket. She leaps on the policeman and koshes him with it. He staggers back, consumed by fiery light. The judge has Oscar by the throat. She tries to unpeel his hands, but the grip is like steel – so she switches on the torch and pushes it so close to his right eye that he falls away with the agonizing dazzle of it. The priest is hanging on to Oscar's legs, yelling the curse of the Church – until the girl shoves the lighted end of the torch into his pontificating mouth. He lets go and runs off, unable to dislodge the light shining down into his own animal guts.

Just time for Oscar to say, 'Thank you, young lady – you're a treasure …' before Apollinaire spots a group of appalling, corseted women trying to strangle Isadora Duncan with her own scarf. With a yell of 'Come on!', Oscar, rapidly recovering from his own ordeal, leads the way … and in no time at all the three of them have sent the women sprawling on the ground in an undignified tangle of orange petticoats and jewellery. Released from their murderous clutches, Isadora dances off bare-footed through the flames.

It's then I hear a terrible wheezing sound. Behind a dark tomb glittering with gilded tributes. I manage to draw the girl's attention to it. 'Quick!' she screams at the others. 'It's Monsieur Proust!'

Two old generals are pinning him down while a third is holding a sprig of pollen-heavy hawthorn right under his nose to trigger an asthma attack.

The girl whips out the gun and aims it at them. 'Stop – or I shoot.'

When I left Lucien's, I had nowhere to go. There was no longer space for me at my aunt's (my cousin was back from the army and needed his room again). My only option was to play the prodigal daughter returning home to the forgiving arms of a loving father. Weren't we all desperate for more love, more security, having just seen what hatred will do? Weren't we all frightened for our beautiful cities?

I still had the key to our apartment. I went back in the middle of the day, when I was less likely to find anyone at home. The thing I wanted most was to curl up in the familiar bed of my childhood, in my familiar room, fall asleep and be woken by the joyful cries and embraces of a father whose happiness returned with the return of his beloved daughter. A fairy-tale reconciliation. I knew how it would be – what I would say. I'd even protected myself by imagining various versions of the scene and rehearsing them in my head. Different scripts – though all variations on a theme of love and healing.

I listened outside the door. Silence. If Madeleine had been at home, there'd be the sound of the radio or TV: she hated silence. But I rang the bell, just in case.

Nothing.

And, no, they hadn't changed the lock.

So odd, to walk back into that life: the dull pictures in the hallway, the muffling carpets, the same heavy drapes at the windows. Heart racing, I went slowly along the passage to the door of my room – which was, predictably, closed.

My body could already feel the relief of throwing itself on to the familiar bed, my eyes could foresee the restful way the light from the long window fell upon my desk at this time of day, my books, the wardrobe door …

My fingers on the familiar curve of the old door-handle ...

But it was the wrong room. How silly. I must've ...

Then I realized. Pierre had taken over my room. None of my things was there any more. Even the furniture had been moved around so my desk wasn't in the usual place and the bed was against the opposite wall ... Instead of books on the shelves, there were videos and cheap-looking sports' trophies and all sorts of other rubbishy bits and pieces. A muddy-legged track-suit in a heap on the floor and some smelly trainers beside it. My desk a mess of tapes and tape-covers, CDs, magazines on motor-racing and football. The bed was unmade – a rumple of stale-looking duvet and pillows.

He'd always been jealous because I had the bigger room (being the elder). With Madeleine on his side, I suppose it didn't take much to persuade my father: two against one.

So much for my fond vision of them keeping my room as a 'shrine' – keeping it as it was in the hope that one day the prodigal would return ... I should've guessed. And this was a version I hadn't scripted beforehand.

The little drawer with the key – the 'secret' drawer on the left-hand side of my desk. Surely they hadn't taken the things out of my desk. The idea of anyone touching my personal things – letters from my friends, postcards, the bits and pieces that mean a lot only to the person that owns them. But most of all I wanted to know if he'd been to my 'secret' drawer – where I kept my poems, and things from my life with Driss ... the napkins from the Chalet des Îles he gave me that day when we took the little boat in the Bois ... reviews of films or books he thought would interest me – just fragile bits of yellowing paper that would be rubbish to anyone else.

I tried the secret drawer. It was locked. Hopeful.

I'd always kept the key to it in the bottom drawer on the right – which I now opened. It was stuffed with a big rolled-up flag – something to do with football, I imagine. My hope was that the small key had stayed there unnoticed when they'd cleared out the old school exercise-books and papers that used to be there. (Had they thrown them away? – or just put them in a box in Pierre's old room?) I pulled the drawer out as far as it would go and felt down behind the flag – which was when my fingers first touched it. Not the key. A large hard object.

It didn't take a genius to realize what it was, just from feeling the shape.

I pulled the flag right out, no longer caring whether my 'intrusion' would be detected, and lifted out the gun. So heavy. And the smell of it.

I looked and felt once more – but the little key had gone – though that scarcely bothered me now.

I couldn't imagine what Pierre was doing with a gun. Did he belong to a shooting club? Would this be the kind of gun they'd use for that? No idea. A number of possible scenarios flashed through my head – one of which was that he – or the person he was keeping it for, maybe? – would use the gun against someone who … (I saw another young man in bandages, another girl keeping a deathbed vigil, her future destroyed …).

I had no idea if it was loaded, no idea how to tell – but I put it in my bag, left the drawer open, the flag in a heap on the floor, then I emptied the filthy remains of three half-drunk cups of coffee over his bed, slammed the door and walked out of the apartment without setting the security lock. I hoped my father would get back first and have an argument with Madeleine about her forgetting to lock up properly – again.

It was unlikely Pierre would say anything about the missing gun, after all.

Proust's eyes widen: in pointing the gun at his attackers, she's also pointing it straight at him.

But it works. The threat of a weapon is a language the generals understand. They jump up and retreat through the turmoil of flames and fighting. Proust recovers his breath sufficiently to wheeze a brief '*Merci … merci …*'

We all duck as we find ourselves in the middle of a pitched battle, with Balzac and Victor Hugo hurling their books at a company of 'respectable' business sharks. A copy of *Peau de Chagrin* misses its target and clips the girl painfully on the back of the neck. Barely flinching, she picks it up and finishes the job for Balzac; it smashes into the face of a property dealer, who staggers away with a severely bleeding nose – and trips over the supine form of his friend, laid low by the hardback edition of *Les Misérables*, now face-up on the ground beside his head.

There's a lot of falling-over going on, and we can't see why – until Oscar spots La Fontaine letting loose from his head hosts of little animals that run between the enemy's legs, tripping them up or nipping their ankles so it's too painful to walk. They sit among fallen comrades, nursing ignominious wounds (one bitten by a tortoise).

Laughing, we flit on through the chaos, try to see where help's needed.

Seurat, perched in a tree, is making excellent work of flicking dabs of paint into hostile eyes – his aim phenomenally precise, a reserved smile on his gentle, courageous face.

With burning eyes and a manic grin, Modigliani releases his exquisite, elongated nudes to distract the enemy and inspire the allies, while Delacroix joyously conjures his 'Liberty' to lead the people once more – a splendid, inspiring figure to revive any flagging spirits ... *'En avant! Vive la liberté!'*

Sarah Bernhardt has unscrewed her wooden leg and is defending herself vigorously against a group of miserable-looking men in black. Does she need help? We look at Oscar: in life, she'd declined to help him when he needed it, despite his adoration of her. He's battling with his conscience: to help, or not to help? But before he can make a decision, the wooden leg has beaten off her attackers and she manages, hoppingly, to reattach it, and hobbles away in happy victory.

Against the orange sky we see the sharp silhouette of the astronomer Laplace: he's on top of the tallest monument, gazing at the stars through his telescope as if nothing were going on down below. And almost at the same moment Apollinaire points to a group of old men who used to be on the Board of Censors stomping straight towards us, wielding their holy books and various bits of gold.

The girl begins to run. She's running away after all. I'm so ashamed.

Let her go. I'll stick with the others ...

But then, with a lurch of pride, I see her. Clambering up the monument, she snatches the heavy telescope from a surprised Laplace and reaches us just in time to use that ideal weapon against the smug huddle of paunchy censors.

Wham! Bam! They're seeing stars and the Church gold flies off in all directions as she picks them off one by one with the wide end of the telescope. 'Take that! – And THAT! ...'

Oscar and Apollinaire bind them together with their own neck-ties, laughing and shouting above the bedlam, 'Well done! Well done, you! You're a marvel! A heroine!'

Suddenly Rossini and Bellini rush past yelling, 'Come and help. They're torturing Chopin.' We follow them, stumbling, dodging round tombs and giving the slip to pursuers. The girl is nimbler than any of us and she's laughing, laughing … I'm so proud of her – so proud …

But before we even get to Chopin, the rescue has begun. It sounds like music to start with – a chord … then more notes added – more and more and more … And without being told I seem to know that it's all the notes of every piece of music ever written by the composers 'at rest' here, every single note played simultaneously, an immense expansion of sound that goes on and on swelling … on and on and on …

The decibels are stupendous, transfiguring …

The enemy are holding their heads, covering their ears, rocking their skulls from side to side … they can't think – can't see – can't do a thing …

And nor can I. The pressure builds up and up inside my head – and as if blood is being forced into the lenses of my eyes, all my seeing turns to red. It makes the sight before me even worse – blood-red figures contorted on the ground between vermilion tombs, mouths open in scarlet agony, heads clasped and rocked in desperate hands, the sound so loud now that it's beyond hearing, beyond *bearing* – louder and louder and louder …

… till the brain registers it as a skull-splitting
silence.

The silence in the room once it was all over. The machines turned off.

After a while his father left. I couldn't look up. I just went on staring at my white hand holding his brown hand. His beautiful, gentle brown hand.

The ineffable silence is driving a wedge between us – between her and me. I want so much to be with her, part of her again, but some irresistible force is pulling me away – pulling me back and slightly above her.

Everything is seen in silence and slow motion. And deep, deep red.

Then, among the figures still writhing on the ground as they try to escape the immeasurable sound of silence, I see one unmoving figure sitting on the modest gravestone of some unknown person. He is sitting very, very still – his stillness emphasized, perhaps, by the writhing movements all around him.

The curve of the back, the angle of the head in relation to it, the lie of the hair – they're familiar but I can't quite place them.

Maybe it's Monsieur Proust ... or is it Apollinaire, just looking a bit smaller because he's sitting down ... Or ...

He's sitting very, very still in the red light.

'Hello!' I call.

There's no response.

'Friend or foe?!' I call – assuming it's a friend, but referring to the scene of battle in which we find ourselves.

The head turns slightly – slowly, as if with some difficulty.

The body half-turns towards me – to the left – lifting the left arm that holds – and seems to offer us – a single, red, deep-red rose.

For a moment, the rose distracts us from the face. *('A face still forming ...')*

It's in the same split second that I take a step towards him, recognize – or think I recognize – his so dearly and deeply beloved face and see Thiers approaching him with a raised rifle-butt ready to bring it down on the gentle brown head.

I aim my gun at Thiers' murderous heart.

The rose is in the direct line of fire.

As he prepares to smash at the beautiful head, my finger squeezes the trigger. At the same moment that he falls, the rose explodes in a shower of blood-red petals that hang in the air a moment, then begin to fall in slow motion, gently. Turning as they fall, they're like poppy petals for Remembrance Day, turning and falling like red snow ...

And the scene draws away from me, encloses itself in a glass globe like the childhood gift, the little snow-scene ... only now the snow is red, the scene is red ...

... and it draws away, away, smaller and smaller, surrounded by darkness, darkness gathering, thicker and thicker ... a choking black dust that marks the place where a story ended ... maybe ...

Blackness and silence.

I've lost the girl in them …

And just as the overwhelming music became silence, so now the consuming blackness becomes light – brilliant white light, like passing through sun-flooded clouds in a plane – a brightness that makes it impossible to see anything.

I want to see her and I can't.

I'm drifting from her … drifting away …

Then I hear her voice – thin but clear.

'Driss! Is it you? Are you there?'

No reply.

'I know you're there. I saw you. I'm sure I did. Stop playing about. It's not funny, you know.'

No reply.

There's silence for a while. I can only imagine how she's wondering – questioning the evidence of her own eyes. Was it him? If she plays along with whatever little game he's invented here and stops calling, maybe he'll come to her, in the end.

She stays quiet – then, unable to bear the silence of the white light any longer, she calls out again. But not to him. She calls the others, maybe hoping he'll hear and be jealous and come to her.

'Oscar – 'Pollinaire! Where are you? I can't see you. I can't see anything.'

But he doesn't come to her.

She calls out to her other friends. 'Gertie … Marcel … I'm frightened. Is it over? … Did we win? … Did I kill that Adolphe? Where are you? I want to be with you. Please. Don't leave me on my own. It's so silent. No voices. No laughing. I don't even know whether I'm dead or alive – dead or dreaming …'

A vague jabbering – but in the misty-white glare, I can't locate the voices for her. I want to bring them to her – to comfort, reassure … But I'm being pulled up through amazing white light

174

… into silence – spread out on to the silence of a blank white page staring for a story.

At last the terrible brightness begins to fade. I look down on the familiar scene, now turning to grey – the tombs, the pathways, wind stirring fallen leaves.

It's dark now, except for a pock-marked moon – which silvers the paths and lights up the little scene beside the Héloïse and Abelard tomb.

The guards. The ambulance men. They're working quickly. In no time at all she's on the stretcher and the ambulance is wailing away through the night.

I'm left here.

The guards yawn on their way back to the office. They'll have to write a report on the incident. I'm curious to know what kind of story they've given her, curious to know what's happened to her, where she's been taken. In case I'll be able to join her …

In case we can continue, the girl and I.

One guard stays outside. I follow the other one inside.

He sits down at the little table and opens the file of reports on security incidents. He pauses, thoughtfully, as if not quite sure what to write on the blank page – though he knows he must start with the date and the time at which the report is being written.

I look over his shoulder. He checks his watch. A hand picks up the pen. It begins.

'1/11: 00.15.'

Nothing more is written for the moment. He's staring ahead. What to put? Wondering whose daughter she is? … Thinking of his own, maybe? … Wondering how, why, this young woman …

I wish I could tell him.

I like to think he would listen.

Acknowledgments

I would like to express my thanks to those involved – directly and indirectly – with the writing of *Zade*. To Mai Ghoussoub and André Gaspard at Saqi, along with Jana Gough, Mitch Albert, Sarah Al-Hamad and Anna Wilson for their excellent editing and always cheerful professional help in every way. To Sara Maitland, Julia Bell, and Rebecca Swift at TLC for all their invaluable suggestions and encouragement in the early stages. To writer friends who gave up precious time to read and offer comments: Marita Over, Jeremy Over, Susie Reynolds, Robert Cole, Dorothy Schwarz, Maggie Freeman. To David Grossman for his general encouragement at a vital time. To Christine Brooke-Rose for her wonderful fictions – especially *Textermination*, which inspired the 'purple cinema' passage in *Zade*.

To my parents, Joan and Albert Simons, for their support in so many ways. To my children, Eduardo and Joanna, who are more central to the story than they may realise. And to others who may or may not know the parts they played: Paula Meehan, Annie Woodward, David Yellop, 'Gabby' and, in France, Agnès Gendre and her family (the Sauvegrains and Robins), and Ada Ruata.

And above all, to my partner, Malcolm Burgess, for his continual faith, encouragement, advice, intellectual companionship, his practical as well as literary help – and for his sustained enthusiasm during those many visits to Père Lachaise. *Zade* is for him, with my love.